[illegible] TO READERS

This book is published by

THE ULVERSCROFT FOUNDATION

[illegible] charity in the U.K. No. [illegible]

The Foundation was established in 1972 to provide funds to help towards research, diagnosis and treatment of eye diseases. Below are a few examples of contributions made by THE ULVERSCROFT FOUNDATION:

A new Children's Assessment Unit at Moorfield's Hospital, London.

Twin operating theatres at the Western Ophthalmic Hospital, London.

The Frederick Thorpe Ulverscroft Chair of Ophthalmology at the University of Leicester.

Eye Laser equipment to various eye hospitals.

If you would like to help further the work of the Foundation by making a donation or leaving a legacy, every contribution, no matter how small, is received with gratitude. Please write for details to:

THE ULVERSCROFT FOUNDATION,
The Green, Bradgate Road, Anstey,
Leicester LE7 7FU. England.
Telephone: [illegible]

SPECIAL MESSAGE TO READERS

This book is published by

THE ULVERSCROFT FOUNDATION

a registered charity in the U.K., No. 264873

The Foundation was established in 1974 to provide funds to help towards research, diagnosis and treatment of eye diseases. Below are a few examples of contributions made by THE ULVERSCROFT FOUNDATION:

A new Children's Assessment Unit at Moorfield's Hospital, London.

•

Twin operating theatres at the Western Ophthalmic Hospital, London.

•

The Frederick Thorpe Ulverscroft Chair of Ophthalmology at the University of Leicester.

•

Eye Laser equipment to various eye hospitals.

If you would like to help further the work of the Foundation by making a donation or leaving a legacy, every contribution, no matter how small, is received with gratitude. Please write for details to:

THE ULVERSCROFT FOUNDATION,
The Green, Bradgate Road, Anstey,
Leicester LE7 7FU. England

Telephone: (0533) 364325

B

STARR'S SHOWDOWN

A drifter with a fast draw and a haunted past, Billy Starr's lean prowess impressed Mike Dunstan, boss of the big No Man's Land spread. Billy landed a job, keeping squatters off the ranch by whatever means he chooses. But he learns that he has sold his soul to the wrong side too late, for Dunstan has plans to keep him on the payroll, or put him six feet under.

G. CLIFTON WISLER

STARR'S SHOWDOWN

Complete and Unabridged

LINFORD
Leicester

First published in Great Britain in 1989 by
Robert Hale Limited
London

First Linford Edition
published October 1991
by arrangement with
Robert Hale Limited, London
and Ballantine Books
(a division of Random House, Inc., New York)

British Library CIP Data

Wisler, G. Clifton (Gary Clifton) *1950* –
Starr's showdown. – Large print ed. –
Linford western library
I. Title
813.54

ISBN 0–7089–7096–6

Published by
F. A. Thorpe (Publishing) Ltd.
Anstey, Leicestershire

Set by Words & Graphics Ltd.
Anstey, Leicestershire
Printed and bound in Great Britain by
T. J. Press (Padstow) Ltd., Padstow, Cornwall

for Aunt Nean, with love

Prologue

THE Cimarron river flowed almost seven hundred miles from its origin in the mesa country of New Mexico and Colorado to its juncture with the Arkansas in what would later become the state of Oklahoma. The Cimarron was a wide, rolling river in the wet season, bringing life to the hard plains country, watering fields that flowered with the fledgling stalks of wheat and corn. In the dry months of summer it wound like a snake through treacherous beds that could become quicksand, a wicked oozing mud that could take a man or a horse to the nether regions without a hint of regret.

In the 1870s the word Cimarron stood for a lawlessness, a wild, reckless world where a man's worth was measured by his strength of character and by the way he handled a repeating rifle and a Colt revolver. A thin strip of territory barely thirty-five miles wide, bounded by the Colorado Territory to the west, the states of Kansas and Texas to the north and south, and by lands assigned by treaty to the Indian nations to the east, it had been created by surveying instruments and maps of government. And into this strip poured all the refuse of the West, all those men who had found the surrounding regions ill suited to their particular way of life.

Following the Civil War, a sort of no-man's-land had come into being there, where sheriffs and marshals and troops were as out of place as a high mountain or a green meadow. In the early seventies, as Texans drove cattle to markets west of the Kansas quarantine line, it became the last free range amid a sea of Kansas and Colorado farmland.

Churches and stores and hotels were unknown in the wild plains country south of the Cimarron. It was a land of scattered trading posts, of saloons and brothels and sod houses used by the roaming cattlemen on their annual pilgrimages to markets in Dodge City on the Arkansas River to the north.

Indians still roamed the region then. Comanches and Kiowas hunted the last dwindling herds of the great hairy buffalo when and where they found them. Cheyenne war parties not massacred with Black Kettle on the Washita two winters before sometimes raided the small settlements and cattle herds. But the Indian, too, was passing from the scene.

Other changes were coming. Even as the bony Texas steers, which got their name from the long wicked horns that jutted dangerously from each side of their heads, established dominion over the country, railroads were creeping ever onward, chopping up the grasslands, bringing railheads into the heart of Texas and Louisiana and Arkansas. Blue-coated soldiers and broad-hatted U.S. marshals began to intrude on the last haunts of the outlaws and cattlemen. The even more feared stinging wire that had already started slicing up the Texas range was spreading across Kansas, and there was talk of statehood for Colorado. Such talk spelled change for the Cimarron country.

To some, change was the greatest enemy of all. To men who'd been born to a land that recognized neither the bounds of a fence nor the limits of the law, changing came hard. Such men were used to a world that allowed a man to own what he could hold, to live only so long as he was stronger than his enemies. A Bowie knife and a revolver, a proud horse and the far horizon: these were the things that he knew and understood. It was enough.

1

THE town of Dodge City huddled along the banks of the Arkansas in southwestern Kansas. Built beside the army post of Fort Dodge, guarding the crossings of the Arkansas River, in 1870 the town had yet to witness the heyday of cattle and violence that lay on the horizon.

Dodge City had law, perhaps the last of it to be found for a hundred miles west and south. But it was best known for its whiskey and women. That was what drew the men sitting inside the Domino Saloon on Front Street.

They were a varied lot. Two old buffalo hunters kept their own company with a bottle in one corner. A saloon girl with a painted face, old at twenty-two, sat across from a clean-shaven man dressed in a fine New Orleans suit. The bartender and owner, Max Green, was one-quarter Kiowa. Just beneath the bar he kept a nine-pound wooden club and a loaded shotgun that preserved the peace in the Domino and ensured payment of all tabs.

In the center of the place was a large round table. Five men were seated there, four of them wearing the trail dust and spurs of Texas cowboys. The fifth was a dark-eyed man in his mid-twenties, sandy-haired and in need of a bath and shave. He wore buckskins, boots made Indian-fashion from buffalo hide, and a tall gray hat bearing the insignia of the Confederate States of America.

Kansas was not known to be friendly to the Southern cause, and such hats were rare, even now that the war had been over for five years. The man in the gray hat appeared unconcerned, though. A huge hunting knife bulged out of a scabbard on his leg, and a long-barrelled Colt revolver hung on his hip.

Anyone who took the time to notice could see that here was a man who had endured hard times. He played his cards tight and close to his chest. His eyes shifted back and forth across the table, watching each of the other players and their nimble fingers.

He was not a man to talk much. The others laughed about Mexican women and fine times in Abilene. The one in the gray hat spoke only to bet or fold or call. And as the night wore on, the money rested mainly between his elbows.

"Uncommon good luck you seem to be having, stranger," the youngest of the cowboys said. "Uncommon."

"Deal the cards, Jim," said a tall, dark-haired man with a heavy mustache. "Play poker."

Cards were dealt, hands were won and lost, and still the eyes beneath the gray hat remained fixed on the table, frozen to the game.

Another man entered the saloon then. He was shorter and, at thirty-six, a bit old for the plains. He wore a black broad-brimmed hat over coal-black hair.

When he smiled, three teeth were seen to be missing from his mouth. A great hook nose dominated his face, giving it a touch of ugliness and an air of cruelty. Even the smile hinted of deceit. He accepted a mug of beer from the bartender while he examined the room.

"Hey, Dunstan," the dark-haired man called from the game table. "Pull up a chair."

"No thanks, boys," the man named Dunstan said. "I've seen this fellow in the gray hat play. He's too good for my blood."

The cattlemen looked again at the ex-Confederate. No emotion appeared on the man's face at all. And the chill in those blue eyes was enough to drive the devil to a warmer climate.

That hand, too, was won by the man in the gray hat, and the deal passed to the young Texan named Jim. The cards were shuffled and cut, then dealt once again.

The betting was brisk that round.

After a single raise, only Jim and the ex-Confederate took cards. The youngster from Texas seemed pleased with his draw, and the pot grew to hold close to two hundred dollars. As the final call was made, the young man spread out three kings. A smile grew from the corners of his mouth.

"Most of the time three kings would beat two pair," the man in the gray hat said. "But it's a strange thing about my two pair. I got myself two sevens," he said, placing them face up on the table, "and two kings."

There was a stir at the table, and Max probed beneath the bar for his shotgun.

"Mister, we don't cheat," the dark-haired cowboy said.

"I'm glad to hear that," the man in the gray hat replied. "Now, I'd like to hear that from young Jim here. Seems to me the king of spades he's got might be a little fresh to've come from our deck."

The ex-Confederate flipped the cards

over, revealing the shiny back of a new card beside two older ones.

"Now *my* spade," he continued, "has got a little age to it. You might keep that in mind next time your sleeve decides to do a little fancy footwork, Jim."

The Southerner began raking in the money, but Jim slammed down a fist.

"We're no different, the two of us, mister!" Jim shouted. "We both cheat. You're just slicker at it."

"Son, you'd best take your hand off my money," the man in the gray hat said. "You learn to play better before you call a man for cheating. That's a loser's play."

"He's just excitable, mister," said the tall man sitting beside Jim. "He's been trailing cows most of a year, and that's his whole showing for it you're taking."

"I never leave a man broke," the ex-Confederate said, shoving fifty dollars at the boy. "I been that way myself."

"I didn't ask for any handout," Jim

said, standing up and pushing his coat back from two shiny revolvers.

"Jim, sit down, for God's sake!" the tall man pleaded.

"I'll defend my own interests," the man in the gray hat said to the others, easing back from the table, his eyes glued to the young man opposite him.

"Your cheating, you mean!" Jim yelled.

"A man who doesn't know about losing shouldn't gamble," Max said from the bar.

One of the cowboys stood up and pointed a pistol at the bartender.

"It's up to the two of them, Max," the drover said. "Even up."

"That right, Jim?" the ex-Confederate asked. "You want to settle this man to man? You make sure these boys know where you want your bones taken, because you won't walk away from this table if you draw your gun on me."

"Big man and tall talk, huh?" Jim asked, his palms sweating. "I've killed men before, two of them in Abilene last month."

"That's a shame," the Southerner said. "If you're fast, I'll be killing you for certain."

The two of them squared off then, circling the table while the buffalo hunters scurried behind the piano, and the other poker players backed to one side.

"Whenever you get the feel for it, you go ahead," the man in the gray hat said. "Wouldn't want anybody to get the idea I took you at a disadvantage."

"Little chance of that," the tall man said, laughing. "Jim's a fine hand with a gun."

The young man drew then, but before his Colt came up level, a shot exploded through the saloon. The man in the gray hat then turned to blast the tall man as his gun was drawn. The cowboy beside the bartender swung a pistol toward the ex-Confederate, then screamed out in pain as the pistol was shot away.

"Anybody else?" the man in the gray

hat asked, shaking slightly. "Come on! You got me in the mood to use this piece. Anybody else want to get back across the Red River the long way?"

The sole remaining cowboy retreated. As the smoke cleared, the man beside the bar nursed a hand with only two fingers and the tall man and young Jim lay on the floor, their eyes, devoid of all life, staring at the ceiling.

"That boy's got a brother in town," the injured drover said. "Bob Smith. He won't like this one bit."

"Then you tell him to look for a man in a gray hat," the Southerner said. "You tell him just who it was shot his brother. I wouldn't want him to have any trouble figuring it out. And you tell him if he's got other brothers, he ought to teach them how to deal cards honest. Some would've shot that boy for the cheating alone."

The two cowboys backed their way out of the Domino, and the ex-Confederate shovelled his winnings into his pockets.

"I'll leave the fifty for the burying," he said, turning to Max. "You tell the boy's brother I'll be around."

"I'll tell him," the man named Dunstan said, stepping forward. Then, with a move as quick as a rattlesnake's, the club came down, and the dark eyes beneath the gray hat closed.

2

THE motionless body of the buckskin-clad stranger rested for a long time in an empty stall at the town's livery stable. There it was safe from the view of a vengeful brother and his friends. At the side of the gambler, the ex-Confederate, the young man who had killed twice and maimed once, sat the menacing figure of Mike Dunstan. Part gunman, part cattle rustler and road agent, part outlaw and renegade, Dunstan was known throughout southern Kansas.

"He's made his pact with the devil, that's for sure," mothers of small children would say, pointing out Dunstan's dark eyes. "Don't be hanging around saloons or playing at cards unless you wish to run across the likes of him."

Dunstan played a strange game of

cat and mouse with the law. He never strayed so far as to attract the attention of the federal marshals, but neither did he let the legality of a thing interfere with his profit.

The young man lying in the hay beside him was a question mark. No one seemed to know him, though he'd been seen by someone playing cards in Abilene several months before.

"He's known the cattle trails," Max had said earlier. "Talked to me once about some herds coming up from Texas on the Chisholm Trail. Seems he came up here that way himself."

"Told me he was up in the Powder River country fighting Sioux Indians," one of the buffalo hunters had related. "He was called Starr or something. Said he did some gold mining in the Montana fields, some more around Denver City."

"Isn't like most gamblers," Rita, the girl who entertained at the Domino, had observed. "He never made a move at me. And his clothes were dusty, like from hard work. You don't get scars like that man has dealing cards, either."

The mystery worried Dunstan some, but not enough to cool his interest in the man's quickness with a Colt.

"Any man who can kill two Texans in the blink of an eye and blow three fingers off another is a man who can be useful," Dunstan mumbled to himself.

Using men was what made money for a man like Dunstan.

It was close to nightfall before the man in the gray hat began to regain consciousness. He started to murmur a name. Ellen, or something like it. There was more, too: a promise to his father. Other names were mumbled low and garbled. And there were places, forts and battlefields and the great rivers of the South and West.

"Hey, you'd best wake up," Dunstan said, shaking him. "Come on now. Let's have no more of that muttering."

The stranger's cold blue eyes finally cracked open. As the light from a lantern cast its glow across his face, he appeared younger than before, almost boyishly innocent. In some ways he was as youthful as the dead Texan who'd chosen the wrong moment to cheat at cards.

"Where am I?" the southerner asked, groping for his pistol.

"Easy now," Dunstan told him. "You're safe and in good hands. We brought you down to the stable."

The ex-Confederate's eyes blinked more than once. He struggled to get to his feet, but a sharp pain between his shoulders blurred his vision.

"You!" he said, clawing at Dunstan with his hands. "You, Dunstan! You hit me!"

"Had to," Dunstan explained. "You'd a been killed."

"Killed, you say?" The stranger laughed. "Not very likely. I can take care of myself."

"Ever hear of a man called Texas Bob Smith?"

"I saw him in Abilene a couple of times. He carries some fancy pistol, a silver-plated model from back East. He doesn't dress sharp, but he can shoot, quick and accurate."

"That boy you shot was Texas Bob's kid brother," Dunstan said. "Bob rides with the Courtney brothers. There's four of them, you know."

"Two," the stranger said. "Calvin and young George got shot in Abilene the week before I left. And the cub – Steve, I think his name is – can't be but fifteen."

"That's still two top guns to face. Harry Courtney must've killed a dozen men now, and Texas Bob, well, he's like poison."

The stranger grinned as Dunstan related the exploits of Texas Bob.

"You ever see Smith shoot?" he finally asked.

"More than once," Dunstan said.

"You tell me, then. Who's faster, me or him?"

Dunstan looked at the cold blue eyes of the man beside him and began to wonder what he'd attached himself to.

Was this a man or a rattler ready to strike at any moment?

"You might take him," Dunstan admitted. "You might take both of them, but where would it get you? The marshal would have you packing your bags. This way ain't much different."

"I never in my life backed away from anybody, Dunstan," the ex-Confederate said, rising.

"Then you're a fool, boy. You don't live long out here until you learn to know the difference between a fight that might bring profit or save your hide and one that'll only go and get you shot full of holes."

"I've been shot before. By Yanks and Indians and white men who said they were my friends. I keep my own company, and I do my own thinking."

The stranger started to gather his things, but Dunstan intervened.

"Listen, maybe we got off on the wrong foot, but I mean to have it different," Dunstan said. "They call me Mike. And you?"

"I've worn a lot of names," the southerner said coldly.

"Those buffalo hunters say you're called Starr."

"Only by the Indians," the man said with an eerie smile. "Lately I've been taking the name of Billy Cook. Suits me as well as another."

"Billy, there's no need for you to hurry off," Dunstan said. "We can get some dinner over at the Front Street Cafe. Maybe we should take a hotel room."

"I thought you were worried about Texas Bob."

"Well, there's two of us to face him and old Harry now," Dunstan said, a cruel smile coming to his lips.

"I don't remember asking you for any favors, Dunstan," Billy Cook said. "I don't need any more whacks on the head."

"Well, then, let's say I owe you one. What would you say to a big Texas steak with a mountain of potatoes and greens?"

"I'm hungry enough, but that'll change nothing. I keep my own company. Tomorrow morning I'll be riding to the Colorado Territory."

"Through the middle of the whole Cheyenne nation?" Dunstan asked. "They're not on good terms with most white men nowadays. Not after Custer rode down on them at the Washita."

"I have no trouble with Indians, Dunstan. Only whites."

"Look, have you got anything pressing up in Colorado? Work, I mean."

"There's always cards to be played in the gold camps," Cook said, putting the dusty gray hat on his head. "And I've still got my pans for stream sifting."

"I know a better way to make the big money," Dunstan said. "Twenty dollars a week and found."

"Doing what? Robbing the stage line?"

"Nothing illegal to it. Ever heard of the Cimarron River?"

"Crossed it more times than I can

remember," Cook said, a faraway look appearing in his eyes. "I lost a good horse to quicksand there once."

"There's a strip of prairie south of the Cimarron, Billy. Nicest range you ever did see. Buffalo used to graze it. Now longhorn steers use it. When the railroad comes to Dodge, Texas herds'll drive up across that strip. It's west of the quarantine line and safer than crossing the nations."

"I've heard of the place," Billy said. "They call it No-man's-land. There's no law there. Nobody owns the range, but everybody claims it. The Colorado people look on it as part of their territory. Comanches hunt a few buffalo there."

"But right now nobody's got clear title to the place. Kansas law can't cross the border, and the rangers out of Texas stay clear as well. Sometimes a real energetic territorial marshal will try his hand, but he usually won't last long. The Daltons ride through from time to time."

"So what would you want me for, an extra gun?"

"Well, I thought you might be a man who thinks like me. I saw those Indian boots you wear, the buckskins. I remember how it was for me as a boy. There were no fences, no judges telling you what you can and what you can't do. There was freedom."

"And now?" Billy asked.

"The strip's the last open range left to a man to run his horses in, to raise his kids. Farmers are moving in. They rob a man of his graze. I aim to keep it open for the herds, and I need help."

"Do the farmers have title to the land?"

"Nobody's got a deed, but who's got a right to it? The likes of them Kansans come down from the Republican and the Smoky Hill, or men like me, who've spent their whole life fighting and dying to keep it free?"

"I don't go chasing people off their land, Dunstan!"

"Didn't ask you to. Just help ride

herd. Keep them that's not wanted off the range. And maybe keep out some of the riffraff we don't need in town."

"I never heard of a town in the Cimarron country."

"Cimarron City, we call it," Dunstan said, smiling. "We've even got a new mercantile with pretty red shutters. More than one saloon's opened up. There's plenty of chances to play cards if a man's got the will."

"Still, there's mountains in Colorado up in Ute country I've never seen," Billy said.

"I tell you what, kid. I got three boxes of Winchester rifles to deliver. Ride with me and there's twenty dollars gold in it for you. You want to ride on to Colorado from there, you do it. It's no farther from Cimarron than from Dodge City."

"That sounds fair enough," Billy said, shaking hands with Dunstan.

He then felt for the money in his pockets.

"All there, even the fifty," Dunstan

told him. "Texas Bob can pay for the burying."

"Well, let's hope he's a while yet in Abilene," Billy said. "I'm hungry, and I mean to have a bath."

"I know just the place," Dunstan said, leading the way.

After eating two huge steaks and soaking for an hour in a hot bath at the Chinese bathhouse, the two men wound their way upstairs to the room they were to share. Dunstan claimed it was the only one available, but his companion suspected the older man didn't wish to risk his having a change of heart.

"Tell me, Billy," Dunstan said as they prepared to go to sleep. "Who's Ellen?"

In a flash the younger man dove onto Dunstan and pinned him with a forearm to the wall.

"Don't you ever mention that name again!" Billy screamed, his eyes full of fury.

"I was only wondering," Dunstan said coolly, filing away in his memory the fact that Billy Cook could be riled. "You said a lot of words in your sleep, but mostly her name."

"It's nothing," Billy said. "I used to know her. I left her behind after the war."

"I meant to say something to you about that, too."

The younger man's neck reddened, and his eyes turned cold and deadly.

"No comments about the Southern cause," Dunstan said. "I was out West at the time myself. I never found any profit in a war. But out here in Kansas, people don't look favorably on a gray hat. You might do better to swap it for something else."

"I'm not ashamed of that hat," Billy said.

"It was your father's, was it?"

"Mine. I was a major in the cavalry. If the war'd lasted another month, I'd a worn a colonel's stars. It was in the works when Richmond fell."

"You don't look to me to be more'n twenty-five," Dunstan said. "How long did you fight in that war?"

"From 'sixty-two on," Cook said proudly. "I joined at fifteen and fought my first battle at sixteen."

"Well, maybe you'll get to fight yourself another," Dunstan murmured, lying down on the bed.

To himself, the old renegade thought that he had indeed found his man. With a little polish and some careful handling, this boy might be another Art Danby. And with three guns fighting for the open range, what farmer stood half a chance to hold his home or his land?

3

THE hotel room faced east, so the morning sun broke through the single window early. The furnishings were bathed in a bright yellow glow, and the men sat up slowly. Dunstan hurried to get dressed, then excused himself.

"I've got to get the rifles loaded onto my wagon," he explained. "I'll meet you downstairs for breakfast in half an hour."

"Sure," the younger man replied from across the room.

As Dunstan closed the door behind him, the man who called himself Billy Cook gazed out the window at the street below.

Images raced through his mind. He'd dreamed of Ellen again. He hadn't seen her since '66, four very long years before. He was dead to her world.

And she was best forgotten, buried like the childhood he'd spent chasing Comanche friends through the waters of the Brazos, like hunting buffalo on the plains and wintering alone in the high country. There was no place to be alone anymore. People had arrived everywhere.

He'd given some thought to Canada. Some said there were places there still untouched by human hands, streams that had never felt the foot of a man. But it was cold there, bitter cold, and he was accustomed to Texas summers that could burn warts off a man's thumb or do his cooking for him without a fire.

If his father had lived, he would have stayed in Texas. He could have run cattle along the river, built a house for Ellen and the children that would have been theirs. But it was a dream lost long ago, erased forever by an ambitious brother and a shadow that brought death and dying everywhere he stepped.

He'd laughed when Dunstan had told

him of how Harry Courtney had killed twelve men. At Fredericksburg he'd shot down more than that one winter's morning. What was the count now, a hundred? There must've been close to thirty since the war, even without counting the Comanches killed along the Brazos or the Sioux up north.

Frowning, he recalled the cattle rustlers on the trail near Wichita, and the man his brother Sam had sent after him in Abilene, and the claim jumpers north of Denver. There'd been gamblers, too, like the day before in Dodge. How many of them? Five or six anyway.

It was bad not to remember them all. A man's dying should make an impression. Most of them were faceless now, shapeless men whose voices still filled his nightmares. He'd likely see them in hell, all lined up beside the devil waiting to greet him.

"Well, old gray hat, you finally made it down here, did you?" they'd say. "We've been waiting for you."

But the way things were, he'd shoot the devil himself if he was cross or had a little liquor in him.

"Hey, Billy, I thought you were going to be halfway through breakfast by now," Dunstan said, appearing in the doorway. "Get your gear together. It's a long ride to the Cimarron, and no white man rides that trail after dark. Not with the Cheyennes talking to their medicine arrows these days."

"The medicine arrows would never be used against two white men travelling alone," Billy said. "They're only taken out when a serious raid is planned."

"What? Are you some kind of expert on Indians or something?"

"I've lived around them most of my life. I hunted with the Comanches as a boy, and I know the ways of the Cheyenne. I passed some time with them, too. Shoshoni and Arapaho, Ute and Kiowa, I know 'em all."

"Then you know we're not on good terms with any of them just now," Dunstan said, frowning. "Let's find ourselves some breakfast and hit the road."

"Sure," Billy agreed.

Billy dressed hurriedly. It wasn't difficult getting into a clean shirt and some fresh trousers. His boots were still dusty from the ride out of Abilene, and he wished there was time to brush them properly. He finally managed to gulp down a quick breakfast of ham and eggs before picking up his big army trunk from the stage depot. He and Dunstan loaded it into the back of the wagon.

"For a man with a dozen names, you don't travel any too light," Dunstan observed. "That's a war chest of sorts."

"It belonged to a friend," Billy said. "He died in the Shenandoah Valley, so I kept the trunk. It's been through some rough times."

"Likely it'll see some more," Dunstan said, whipping the mules into action.

The two men rode southward. Billy had tied his fine horse Comanche to the rear of the wagon. From time to time he glanced back to make sure the proud black stallion was still behind them. It had taken close to a month to catch and train that animal. Billy meant to keep him.

"What kind of a name is Billy Cook?" Dunstan asked as they rolled along the trail. "Did you steal it from some poor fellow or just make it up yourself?"

"Well, I always had a fondness for the name Billy," the young man admitted. "I've thrown in several last names, but Cook's an easy one to remember. And common names people don't take so much note of."

"It'll never do for the kind of work we'll be doing, though. Nobody ever heard of Billy Cook. You need something to put a scare into a man. Where are you from?"

"Here and there," Billy said. "Everywhere at one time or another."

"Well, we can't call you after all of them. Virginia or Mississippi wouldn't do at all. You say you rode with the Comanches for a time. How about the Comanche Kid?"

"There's a Comanche Kid with two thousand dollars on his head. I aim to stay alive longer than he will."

"Well, any old place'll serve. Why not the Cimarron? How would that be, the Cimarron Kid?"

"I picked Billy Cook."

"It'll never do," Dunstan said. "Sounds too innocent. People don't get the jitters from a name like that."

"It's not the name that does the shooting," Billy told him.

"If you've got a big enough name, you don't have to do so much shooting," Dunstan explained. "That's the idea. We don't mean to kill every farmer between here and Texas. We'll just suggest they move on along."

"And?"

"Billy Cook alone isn't going to move anyone. You say you've been called Starr? How about that?"

"You're doing the talking."

"When we get to town, we'll be finding you a better outfit, too. Maybe white leather, big black boots. A new gun, too."

"I like this one," Billy said.

"It's got too long a barrel to be handy," Dunstan said, shaking his head.

"Look, I put this piece together myself," Billy said, drawing the weapon out of its holster and turning it over in his hands. "It's the finest pistol for shooting at under a hundred yards you ever saw. It's fast firing, and it never jams. It gets the shot where you want it, too."

"The shooter does that mostly," Dunstan said, using Billy's own argument.

"Not unless he's got a gun that responds. No, the Colt stays with me. So does the hat."

"I'm telling you, Starr, that hat's pure stupid. Texas boys won't take it well, you being so young and an officer in the war. And Yanks, especially the army and the marshals, will take a hard look at you 'cause of it."

"Let 'em," Billy said. "I like being seen."

"Well, it does make you look a little reckless. That's not without merit, and maybe they'll figure a kid who fought in the war is just a little meaner than they might otherwise suspect."

"I'm glad that's all settled." Billy sighed.

The two men rode close to twenty miles that day. In a wagon it was more than a hard day's travel, and they slept well and in peace that night. When morning came, though, they discovered company had arrived.

"Get up, Starr!" Dunstan shouted. "Indians!"

Billy rolled out of his blankets and searched the horizon. Sure enough, three figures on horseback stood some twenty yards away.

"Kiowas," Dunstan said, fumbling around for his gun.

"You know Indians, do you?" Billy asked.

"I know Kiowas," Dunstan answered. "I've crossed trails with 'em before."

"But not often in the daylight, huh?

Kiowas like to wear feathers in a line from their foreheads across to the back of their heads. Not like these bucks. They've got painted buckskin bands across their foreheads, and they're short for Plains Indians. No, these are Comanches."

"This far north?"

"They once roamed as far as the Platte, Dunstan. They're likely stalking game, or they came up to take a look at what's happening around Fort Dodge."

"You figure they'll take an interest in us?"

"Depends," Billy said. "If they know what's in the wagon, I'd say they'll be attentive enough."

Dunstan's face turned a little pale. Billy laughed and walked out to meet the visitors, holding his right hand in the air to show he held no gun.

"You are without company, white man," the Indian in the middle called to Billy.

"But we have excellent company now Red Hawk," Billy replied.

"You call me by the name I was given long ago," the Indian said, showing surprise. "I am now called Sky Speaker."

"Sky Speaker, you are welcome in my camp," Billy said, motioning toward the wagon. "I have some tobacco I'll share with you, but I'm poor in horses and have no present to make to you."

"Ah, it is that way with me, too," Sky Speaker said. "It is not a good year for horses or buffalo. We travel far from the ranges we hunted before."

"There are soldiers on the Arkansas," Billy told them. "I've seen them ride so that the dust from their hooves robs the light of the sun."

The three Indians exchanged worried looks.

"I have seen you before," Sky Speaker said. "Many summers past you hunted with my uncle, Yellow Shirt. He comes no more to the buffalo hunt. His sons we never see now."

"They are all dead, even the last of them," Billy said, sadly, recalling how as a boy he'd hunted deer with Red Wolf, Yellow Shirt's son.

"I have heard this," Sky Speaker said. "I was told the one called Star by the light of day killed many of my brothers in a time of great darkness."

"I've killed Comanches," Billy said, squaring his shoulders so that he appeared stiff and unyielding. "The treaty oak was cut, and war came to the valley. Just as you would guard the lodge of your brother, so I did for mine."

"Now you ride with that one, Star," Sky Speaker said, pointing to Dunstan. "You have lost your way, I think."

"I ride from the town up north," Billy explained. "I killed two of my enemies there, but they have friends. I've killed enough. My spirit is troubled. I need time to myself."

"Do you ride to the great river now, Star?" Sky Speaker asked. "Would you leave this place to the Comanche and our brothers, the Kiowa?"

"I'd leave you all the land, just

as you'd leave it to me," Billy told the Indians, making motions with his hands as he did so. "My arm still bears the mark left by a Comanche lance, given me in my fourteenth summer. And my wrist still shows the mark of Yellow Shirt's knife, a reminder of the time my blood mixed with that of the Comanche."

"Red Wolf is dead," Sky Speaker said angrily. "It has been a long time since the blood of a white man flowed through Comanche veins. Star, you carry guns that will kill my people. This should not be. Give me these guns."

"If you seek guns for hunting, go to the fort on the Washita and ask the soldiers. If you would take the guns I carry, return painted for war."

"This is the talk we hear from your brother, the one with the angry eyes who sends riders to kill our women," Sky Speaker said with a reddened face. "We do not forget such things."

"I don't walk my brother's path," Billy said, looking intently into the eyes of the Comanche. "I go alone, blown by the wind as the sun and the stars are. Where I come and go is not my choice. Those I kill are not of my choosing."

"This one you ride with is a bad man, Star. His heart is dark with the murder of many Kiowa. He came to their camp in darkness to shoot the women and the little ones."

"I wouldn't know about that. I do know you speak the truth. I'll talk to him about it."

"Will you let us kill him?" Sky Speaker asked.

"No," Billy said. "He rides with me, so you must strike both of us down. You know the power of my medicine, Sky Speaker. You remember the boy who struck down the buffalo with his lance. You know the spirits spoke to me in Yellow Shirt's camp."

"All this I know, Star, but I also talk with the spirits. This man will blacken your heart. And one day he will kill you."

"No man lives long, Sky Speaker," Billy said, sighing. "Not even a star lives forever."

"You are a bright star no more," the Indian said, angrily turning his horse away. "Your medicine is still strong. We will not fight you this day."

"I don't hide myself," Billy told them. "I won't be hard to find."

"You still have courage," Sky Speaker said, looking back into Billy's eyes. "You may need it."

Sky Speaker then signalled to his companions, and the three Comanches rode off toward the west.

"What did they want?" Dunstan asked when Billy returned to the wagon.

"You, I think," Billy said. "They said you killed some Kiowa women and children. Lucky for us these were Comanches. Kiowas would've ridden us into the ground. Killing a woman! When did you do that?"

"Back in my trading days," Dunstan said, laughing.

"There's nothing funny about it,"

Billy said. "They know we're carrying guns. We might see some more of them before we reach the Cimarron."

"Why didn't they just take the rifles?"

"They're afraid."

"Of the guns?" Dunstan asked.

"Of me," Billy said, rolling up his sleeve. "When I was small, I used to visit the Comanches near my home. I was still a boy when I received this scar from the son of Chief Yellow Shirt. I was praised for my courage. I rode to the buffalo hunt with them. I killed one with a lance. Then I had a dream that led us to a large herd. This is great medicine to them, and they fear it."

"Bunch of nonsense," Dunstan said, shaking his head.

"Is it?" Billy asked. "Sky Speaker sees things, too. He told me something to keep in mind."

"About us?"

"That's right, Dunstan. Now let's get going," Billy said, rolling up his blankets.

They gathered up their belongings and hitched the team to the wagon. Billy mounted Comanche and led the way southwest. Dunstan followed with the wagon.

They crossed another twenty-five miles that day. The two men mounted a watch that night, wary of the Comanches' return. The third day's camp was on the Cimarron River, and the following morning they crossed to the south bank.

Only when the small town of Cimarron City was in sight did the men breathe easier. But even then Billy felt a shadow of the past falling across his path.

4

THEY hardly paused while passing through the fledgling town of Cimarron City. Seeing the place as a city required imagination. Six simple wooden buildings were clustered around a dusty rutted cattle road.

"It's the perfect kind of town," Dunstan said, pointing out each building in turn. "There's a mercantile, livery and smithy, a cantina, and three saloons."

"Hardly a town," Billy grumbled.

"That bother you?" Dunstan asked.

"No, I've seen my share of towns. Let's get on with it."

Dunstan whipped the animals, and the wagon lurched forward. An hour or so later they arrived at a large house atop a low hill. To one side was a long building made of mesquite planks. To the other stood a large barn, badly in need of a fresh coat of paint.

"Was a farm once," Dunstan said. "We kind of took it over."

"How do you kind of take something over?" Billy asked. "That's akin to kind of killing somebody. What happened to the people who lived here, built this place?"

"Ran off to Colorado, I expect. Now cut the chatter and follow me."

Dunstan pulled the wagon to a stop in front of the big house. Then he climbed down from the seat and led the way up several wide stone steps to a huge oaken front door.

"Well, it's Dunstan," a tall, broad-shouldered man announced from the doorway. "Just in time for dinner."

"Mr. McNally, might I introduce Billy Starr," Dunstan said. "I found him in Dodge, shooting it out with three Texans across a card table."

McNally eyed Billy suspiciously. There was more than a trace of doubt in the man's eyes.

"You serve in the army?" McNally asked.

"Four years in Tennessee and Virginia," Billy said.

"Well, Billy, why don't you come along in," McNally suggested. "I can tell you've had an eventful trip down from the Arkansas. Mrs. McNally has a fine supper fixed, and there's a bath waiting for you afterward in the bunkhouse."

"That sounds just about perfect to me," Billy said, taking off his hat and forcing a smile to his face.

"I could stand some dinner myself," Dunstan said, closing the door.

Mrs. McNally seemed out of place in such hostile country. She wore a white lace gown, with a real diamond necklace around her neck. Her manners reminded Billy of the fine ladies of Richmond, of the mansion in Corinth where his wounds had been treated after Shiloh.

"Tell me, Billy, when were you last in the East?" the woman asked. "I never get news."

"I haven't been there since the war, ma'am," Billy told her. "I've been wandering since then."

"Ever worked cattle?" McNally asked. "Longhorns are mean and hard on a man who doesn't know his craft."

"I've been up the trail from Texas," Billy said. "In 'sixty-six before the road was marked. I grew up with cows and horses. I was riding mustangs at four, roping at six. And when you're in the cavalry, you learn to sit a horse and stay there."

"I see," McNally said. "What do you have in mind for this boy, Dunstan? Tending the horses?"

"That would be a waste of good talent," Dunstan said. "Danby handles the town these days, but we've got nobody on the range. I figure to offer Starr here twenty a week to keep an eye on our interests out there."

"Twenty a week?" McNally gasped, standing. "Why, I don't give my own boys that much."

"You don't have to," Dunstan said.

"Besides, those boys of yours can't shoot like Starr. He's good, and he knows it. I watched him make four hundred dollars just playing cards in Dodge. Seems a man with talent ought to get his due."

"I don't know, Mike," McNally said. "It's going to make for some bad blood."

"Then why worry about it?" Billy asked. "I can go to Colorado. I feel better in the mountains anyway. I do thank you for the fine meal, ma'am, but I'd be more comfortable on the road."

"Sit down, Starr," Dunstan said. "Look, Mr. McNally, I didn't bring this kid down from Dodge to keep me company. He's good, better'n anybody I've seen since Danby. He don't drink heavy, and he's got no posters out on him. Better still, he's not known around here yet. That gives us an advantage."

"Word gets out on a fast hand quick enough," McNally said. "I wouldn't expect to find one in a Dodge City saloon."

"Stroke of fortune, if you ask me," Dunstan said. "Anyway, you owe him. We were trailed by Comanches coming down from Dodge. They'd have taken me without thinking twice, but Starr spoke with 'em, called those bucks by name. Had those Indians shaking in their moccasins. A man who knows Indians is worth something. And you got three crates of Winchesters that might be in Comanche hands right now if he hadn't been along."

"You didn't say anything about that before," McNally said. "You know the Plains tribes, do you, Billy?"

"I grew up around the Comanches," Billy explained. "I've lived with Cheyennes and Arapahos. I'll treat with them for you, but I've shot all the Indians I plan to. Ever."

"Nobody on the open range goes hunting Indian trouble," McNally said. "The way it is, any one of those tribes could ride us right into the dust."

"Then it's settled," Dunstan said. "Twenty a week plus the usual bonus.

He gets a horse and a Winchester. He's got his own pistol, one he's partial to."

"Saw it," McNally noted. "Has a long barrel for a Colt."

"I designed it for accuracy across a distance," Billy explained.

"Doesn't it make your draw a little slow?" McNally asked.

"Some might think so," Billy said, glancing at Dunstan.

"I do wish you men would talk of something civilized," Mrs. McNally complained. "Guns and steers, Indians and soldiers. It does seem to me that's all we hear now that Sharon's gone to school."

"Well, ma'am, that's about all there is to life out here," Dunstan said, laughing.

"I wish we had a church in town." She sighed. "Miss Jessica and Molly Carter are in favor."

"We've talked this out before," McNally said. "Churches and schools draw farmers. You've got your prayer book, and I put a chapel down by the pond. That'll have to suffice."

"If we had a church, your sons wouldn't be so wild," the woman said, frowning.

"It's wild country, ma'am," Dunstan told her. "Can't expect a tame man to live too long here."

"It's a poor place to raise a family," Mrs. McNally said, rising from the table. "Poor, indeed."

"I hope I didn't say anything," Dunstan said after she'd left the room.

"No, Mike, she's just upset because Jason's taken to wearing a sidearm. She doesn't understand out here a boy's a man at seventeen," McNally said.

"I see," Dunstan said, smiling. "So now there's another fast-drawing McNally around. Well, I'd best watch my step. You, too, Starr."

Mrs. McNally returned a short while later, carrying bowls of peach cobbler on a small tray. The men dove into the dessert. They were nearly finished eating when two young men in their late teens walked in.

"You're late, boys," McNally said. "We've got company."

"Hello, Mike," the eldest boy said, shaking Dunstan's hand. "Who's this?"

"Billy Starr," Dunstan said. "Starr, meet John and Jason McNally."

"Glad to meet you," Billy said, shaking their hands.

"Sorry we're so late, Ma," Jason said as his mother brought out food for them. "We had a lot of strays out in the north canyons. Something must've spooked 'em. Tomorrow young Bennett ought to ride out there and stay with 'em. He's got nothing better to do."

"Bennett's a good man, Jason," McNally said. "He's seen more cattle than you ever will. I like those Texas boys. They can eat dust and buffalo chips, and the heat doesn't bring 'em down like these Yanks you find hereabouts or up in Dodge."

"What's he going to be doing?" John asked, pointing to Billy. "I never heard of any Billy Starr."

"He's riding the range," Dunstan

said. "Maybe he can pair up with Bennett."

"What is he, another Texas wrangler?" John asked.

"He's anything we need," Dunstan answered. "He's proven himself to me."

"He's the other man you were looking for, the new Danby," Jason said. "How much are we paying him?"

"Twenty a week plus bonus," McNally told them.

"That's more'n I get," John said angrily. "You show me what he can do that I can't!"

"Can you talk Comanche Indians away from a wagonload of Winchesters?" Dunstan asked. "Can you shoot three Texans down in a gunfight? Have you been up the Chisholm Trail?"

"You know I haven't," John said. "But I can outshoot him. I'm sure of that."

"There's one way I know to find out," Dunstan said, smiling wickedly.

"I'll have no shooting on this ranch!" Mrs. McNally said, fear filling her eyes.

"We can still find out," Dunstan said. "We can have a contest. What do you say, Starr? Shoot for sport?"

"I don't have to prove anything," Billy said, finishing his cobbler. "I think I'll take that bath now."

"Wait a minute, Starr!" John said. "Are you turning away from me?"

"I don't shoot at kids," Billy said, scowling. "I give 'em a chance to get a little smarter."

"Starr, just a little demonstration," Dunstan suggested. "Your monthly wage against John's."

Billy smiled a bit at the notion.

"That's more to my liking," he told them. "Anybody else interested in making a wager?"

"Sure, I'll put up fifty dollars you can't take John with a handgun," Jason said.

"Has he got the money?" Billy asked.

"He's got it!" McNally said.

"Then I'll leave it to you, Mr. McNally, to decide what's a fair contest. And to judge things."

“Sound fair to you, John?” McNally asked his son.

“Sure, Pa,” John told him.

After the McNally boys finished their dinner, all five men walked to an empty corral. Dunstan placed two rocks atop the rail, then pointed to them.

“Draw and shoot the rock,” he said. “You first, John.”

John McNally faced the rail, drew out his pistol, and fired. The rock flew up into the air, and Jason clapped.

“Is this once only or best of three?” Billy asked.

“Once only if you miss, Starr,” John said, laughing.

“Then I tell you what,” Billy said. “Put three of them up there. I’ll hit ’em all right now.”

The others stared at Billy for a moment. Then Dunstan stood two more rocks on the rail and backed away.

“I’ll hit ’em left to right,” Billy explained.

Dunstan shouted then, and the long-barreled Colt flashed into action. Faster than a man might have thought possible, the three rocks flew off the rail. Billy then whirled and shot a can off the porch, knocked a limb from a nearby cottonwood, and hit the rooster's tail on the weathervane on top of the barn.

"That was just a little extra, free of charge," Billy said. "Now somebody throw a rock over the corral. We'll shoot till one of us misses. Okay?"

"You go first this time, mister," John said, rubbing his palms on his trousers to dry off the sweat.

"Glad to," Billy said. "Just give me a few minutes to reload."

After Billy had filled the six chambers of his pistol with fresh powder and ball, he replaced the used percussion caps with shiny new ones. Then he motioned to Dunstan. A rock flew into the air. Billy waited for it to start its downward flight, then blasted it into fragments.

"He's a shooter, all right," McNally observed, eyeing his sons.

Dunstan threw a second rock, and John fired. The shot went wide, but a second shot knocked it crazy. The spectators gazed at Billy, who'd drawn and fired in the blink of an eye.

"I didn't want anyone to claim the second rock was harder to hit than the first," Billy said, shrugging his shoulders.

"You'd best keep your guard up, mister," John said, glaring at the newcomer. "Nobody gets the best of me."

"That must be 'cause you've run across some pretty poor competition," Billy said, laughing as Jason handed over the wagered amounts.

"I'll have no more such talk, Billy," McNally said. "You get that bath you talked of. Boys, you go inside. It was a fair contest, and the winner's got his reward."

Then Dunstan led Billy to the bunkhouse.

"You made yourself an enemy tonight," the older man noted. "That John McNally's got a temper."

"He's got some respect now though,"

Billy said. "Now he knows he's a dead man if he draws his pistol on me. Might have cost him a month's wages, but that's cheaper than a month in a sickbed. Or worse."

"Well, here it is," Dunstan said, opening the door of the long wooden building. "I'll get Miguel, the stable boy, to bring you some hot water for the bath. And say hello to Wade Bennett. You'll be working with him."

Dunstan then turned back toward the house, and Billy entered the bunkhouse alone.

5

BILLY found the bunkhouse dark and uninviting. A single lantern burned in the back corner, so he wandered in that direction. Two beds were furnished with blankets, and at the foot of one stood Billy's weathered army chest. A short distance away was a wooden bathtub.

Billy glanced around for Bennett, but no one was nearby. He finally sat on the bed and shook off his boots. A young Mexican boy came in with two buckets of hot water, and the tub was made ready.

"I saw you shoot, señor," the boy said as Billy slipped into the tub. "You got the eye."

"Some say so," Billy told him.

The boy poured water into the tub, and Billy sighed as the warmth penetrated his weary bones.

"I never see many of the ranch hands use this tub," Miguel said. "Me, you couldn't catch me in one of those things, señor. I go to the creek to wash myself."

Billy laughed, then started scrubbing off the dirt.

"You like it here?" Billy asked.

"Señora McNally, she is a good woman. She don't make life so hard on me, and she bakes sometimes. The old man is not so bad. But the boys, ay, they belong to the devil, señor. And the one with the dark hair, Señor Dunstan, I would not trust him so very much."

"Don't listen to everything you hear from a pup of a Mexican kid," a young man remarked, walking through the door and over to the beds.

"He ask me, Señor Bennett," the boy said, collecting his buckets and heading for the door.

"You sure spooked him," Billy said to Bennett. "They call me Billy Starr."

"Wade Bennett," the other man answered. "Glad to see you. It's been a little quiet hereabouts. As to Miguel, it doesn't take much to shake him. His pa and two brothers used to work some land east of here. I heard Danby and Dunstan showed up one day. The next day Miguel was digging graves."

"I'm not sure I like what I'm hearing."

"You'll hear more. I never listen to much of it, though. Mr. McNally is a fine man to work for. He knows stock, and he's generous with his payroll."

"Seems so," Billy agreed.

"Dunstan arrived with Danby about six months ago," Wade said, sitting on his bed. "We were having trouble with rustlers. We'd ride out one day and find some family of squatters just plopped down at one of the water holes, barbecuing a steer or else stealing our horses.

"We had a bunch that came out from Arkansas, stringing wire to cut us off from the river. There's not any law here, and there's no right or wrong most of the time. Mr. McNally was here first and, the way I look at it, that makes this land his."

"This Danby, he's a tall, thin fellow?" Billy asked.

"That's him," Wade said.

"I saw him in Abilene three years ago. He's quick, but he dips his shoulder just before he draws."

"The dip's there, Billy, but he's a killer. I guess he's shot three or four men while Dunstan's been gone. Dunstan doesn't believe in shooting unless there's a profit in it, but Danby'd as soon shoot you as say good morning."

"And McNally's boys?"

"I caught your show," Wade said, laughing. "Watch that John. He's got a mean streak: Jason's all right. They can both shoot, but I haven't seen anything from them I'd call a cattleman's craft. Both of 'em's lazy."

"And you're not?"

"I was raised in McLennan County, Texas, real close to Waco on the Brazos River. By the time I was ten, my brother and father were dead with the Second Texas at Vicksburg."

"Austin Bennett," Billy mumbled.

"That was my brother's name," Wade said. "I saw your hat. You serve with Pemberton?"

"No, but I was with the Second Texas for a time. My father was killed at Shiloh, and I got myself laid up in the hospital. Then I got a commission to ride with the cavalry up Virginia way."

"Pa used to write sometimes about the regiment. Austin, too. I don't remember any Starrs."

"I wasn't too old at the time," Billy said, growing nervous.

"It's not your real name, is it? Don't fret. I'm about the only one around here who still calls himself what his ma wrote in the family Bible. My uncle works the main herd. Clark Bennett's his name. I came down here with him after our trail boss got himself shot in Abilene last year. Mr. McNally was hiring, and it seemed better'n riding all the way back to Jacksboro."

"I thought you said you were from Waco."

"Well, I took to moving around a lot," Wade said, lying down. "I used to help out on the cook's wagon, back when I was twelve or so. By the time I was fourteen I'd hit the trail as a drover. I used to catch a lot of ragging on account of my size, but when you do a man's job, the laughter has a way of dying away."

The memory of a slightly built young man shouldering a heavy musket on the long march across Louisiana to Corinth crept through Billy's mind, but he shook it away.

"Guess I'd best get out of this tub," Billy said finally. "I feel like a piece of waterlogged oak."

"Here," Wade said, reaching over to toss Billy a linen towel. "Bet you feel a bit more human. It's a good thing. Dunstan's sending us out in the morning to round up strays and watch the range."

"Know where I can locate a good cutting horse, Wade?" Billy asked as he dried himself. "Mine's a fine runner, but he's never chased cows."

"You can ride Bluebonnet. She's a fine little pony. You're entitled to a horse, and she's the best around. I broke her myself. And if there's trouble, she can ride all day. She has spirit."

"Sounds good," Billy said. "When you gentled her, you left her a nose for running, didn't you?"

"This is another Texan you're talking to, Billy Starr, or whoever you are. I don't use a whip on a horse. I sleep with him, talk to his soul. I get him so he can smell me and feel me and know what I'm thinking before I do."

"You didn't learn that in Waco," Billy said, shaking his head.

"No, I came onto it by accident. Clark and I had just come back from Kansas. We fell into running with a lot of boys from Jacksboro. It turned out one of them had some work on his place, so we spent a winter there, rounding up mustangs and readying them to be ridden."

"There used to be a lot of horses in Jack County."

"You know the country? Well, it's mostly fenced now. Shame. Anyway, Mr. Cobb – "

"Cobb?"

"You know the man?"

"Did once," Billy said, fighting to control his trembling fingers.

"Well, they say it's a small world. I trailed with Travis Cobb and his brothers all the way to Abilene. Then Clark went with the Donahue brothers. They got themselves shot, though."

"You stayed with the Cobbs?"

"Yeah," Wade said. "You know, Travis served with the Second Texas, too. I'll bet you knew him in the war."

"We rode together in Virginia, too."

"Figure that!" Wade said, whooping.

"Tell me what you can about Travis," Billy said, his heart pounding.

"He got himself married. He had two little girls the last I heard. That was a year ago in Abilene."

"Do you remember anyone else from around there?"

"To tell the truth, I never got along all that well with Travis's brother Les. He's a little like John McNally. He took a bullet in the hand from somebody a few years back, and it's like he's still trying to get even."

"That doesn't surprise me." Billy sighed. "He was excitable even as a boy."

"Billy, you want to know about the sister, don't you?" Wade asked. "Ellie."

"Ellen," Billy mumbled.

"Well, she was keeping house for her pa when I first got there. Pretty girl, I tell you. About a year later she got herself married to a young doctor over in Wise County. I hear she's doing just fine."

Billy shuddered, and his smile faded.

"You don't appear too happy to hear that."

"No, I am. I was just remembering something."

"Yeah, all this talk of home can get to you."

"Sure can," Billy said, pulling on his nightshirt.

The two young men fell silent then, and the crickets took over. Their chirping drowned out a man's thoughts, even the croaking of the bullfrogs from the pond.

Billy opened his trunk and began sifting through its contents.

"What's this?" Wade asked, sitting beside the trunk. "A sword?"

"It's a beauty," Billy said, holding it out for his companion to see. "It belonged to my grandfather originally. He served with Colonel Fannin at Coleta Creek and was shot by the Mexican army at Goliad. My father carried it at Shiloh."

Then Wade drew a beautiful blue cloth from the trunk. As he spread it out on the bed, both men lost their breath. It held a large single white star in the center, surrounded by olive branches.

"I remember seeing that flag in Houston," Wade said. "It was when Pa marched off to war. That's the battle flag of the Second Texas."

"I carried it with me to Virginia," Billy recounted. "And I brought it home with me afterward."

"Your name's not Starr," Wade said, shaking. "That hat and now that flag. You'd better be careful. Stay clear of Texans. You ought to burn this, too," he said, holding out a piece of leather torn from an old boot. It bore a strange brand, the mark of a three-pronged fork.

"I haven't let many men see what's inside here," Billy said.

"They all think you're dead," Wade said. "I heard Travis tell his sister. You'd best be careful. That brother of yours is worse'n five Dunstans."

"I know," Billy mumbled.

"Why didn't you go back?" Wade asked, his eyes wide with curiosity.

"You've got lands that belong to you."

"Well, Wade, it came down to killing a brother, and I couldn't do it. I've done some things in my life I'm not proud of, but never anything like that. You can't build a life on somebody else's dying. So I headed into the mountains. It got lonely sometimes, but there are worse ways to live."

"How come you don't use your own name?"

"Partly I don't want Ellen to hear of it. I guess, too, my brother still might be a bit uncomfortable, not knowing where I am or what I'm up to. But I suppose more than anything it's because I haven't lived up to my father's name."

"But you still carry his sword."

"I guess deep down I still have this dream of finding a place that suits me, somewhere I can ranch a little, make a home for myself, and pass the sword on to my sons."

"If you ever come to need a foreman, let me know," Wade said, smiling broadly.

"I'll do that," Billy told him.

Billy returned the flag to the trunk and slipped under his blankets. Wade blew out the lantern. As the darkness settled in all around them, Billy felt the memories returning.

"She's got a little boy now, Billy," Wade whispered. "I hear they called him William."

"Sorry to hear that." Billy sighed. "I was hoping one of us might have forgotten."

"Seems to me there's some comfort in knowing somebody out there loves you," Wade said.

"Not really," Billy said. "That makes you soft in a way, vulnerable."

For a long time Billy lay awake, staring at the wooden roof of the bunkhouse. His mind was engulfed by recollections of other times, of Ellen's soft hands, of her gentleness. Then the terrible chills that filled every night he spent alone arrived, and he shuddered.

"Oh, Ellen," Billy whispered. "I miss you so much."

Still the memories swept over him, even as clouds of slumber gathered to sweep his consciousness away.

"Ellen, I miss you every night," he said. "Every cold and lonely night."

6

AN hour before daylight Billy walked past the barn to a second corral. Inside, three young stallions and a buttercup mare were running along the rail fencing. A tall, sandy-haired man sat on the rail.

"Billy, this is my uncle Clark," Wade said, pushing Billy toward the man. "Clark, meet Billy Starr."

Billy shook hands with Clark, then examined the horses.

"Billy knows the Brazos country," Wade told his uncle. "So I guess we best pick him out a good mount. Wouldn't want a Texan riding one of these scrub bush ponies you buy in town."

"No, sir," Clark said. "We've got a couple of fair cow ponies here, though."

"I see," Billy said, whistling to one of the stallions.

"The mare's Bluebonnet," Wade

explained. "She's small and wiry, but she'll run the others into the dust."

"I'm not as light a load to carry as you are, Wade," Billy said. "And I can run a horse hard. I'm accustomed to large, strong-winded horses that don't grow shy if a pistol ball's flying by their ear."

"Bluebonnet's not trained to gunfire, but she'll do as you say," Clark said, jumping down from the fence and approaching the mare. "She doesn't panic in a storm or stampede, and she knows her way around the range."

"Well, then, let's try her," Billy said. "You about ready to hit the trail, Wade?"

"You know it," Wade said. "To tell the truth, I don't care much for bunkhouses. I'm a man for the open sky."

"It's out there waiting for us," Billy said.

Wade and Billy gathered their ropes and saddled up. After bidding Clark a brief farewell, they mounted the horses and raced each other across the broad Cimarron plain, spreading a mountain of dust that choked the morning sky behind them.

"Hold up there, Wade Bennett from McLennan County," Billy called to his companion. "I'm not running through the Brazos this morning."

"Showing your age, Billy?" Wade said, grinning.

"How old are you, anyway?"

"Twenty. You thought me older, I'll bet. Pa always said I had an old face."

"But a young heart, huh?" Billy added. "I've still got a ringing in my ears left over from Dodge City. Let's take it a bit easier. What are we doing out here, rounding up strays?"

"So Mr. McNally thinks," Wade said, smiling. "But there's no point to keeping a tight herd when we're not taking the stock anywhere till spring. We're mainly seeing to it no one's hitting the herd or settling the range."

"Rustlers and squatters, in other words."

"That's the bill. But in truth we don't do much but ride around and keep a campfire so people know we're here."

"And if we see somebody busting the range with a plow?"

"Then I'll show you how to get a farmer to change his mind as to where he'll make his home," Wade said, laughing.

The two men rode close to fifteen miles before stopping. There was a fine water hole with shade just ahead, and the horses were growing tired.

"Never hurt to rest from time to time," Wade said. "Might be a good place to camp."

"Water for the horses and fish for supper," Billy said, looking the place over. "Good grazing, too."

"I've shot rabbits here," Wade remarked. "When the grass is high, you can catch a quail or two."

"Then this is the spot to pitch camp. I'm partial to bobwhite."

"I've got a taste for 'em myself," Wade said, smiling.

The two men sat beneath a tall oak and watched the horses drink. The sun had already begun to bake the ground with its late-summer rays. Billy wiped sweat from his forehead and glanced at his friend. Wade had a worried look, and Billy couldn't help wondering about it.

"Something bothering you?" he finally asked.

"Not really." Wade sighed. "I've got something on my mind to say to you, but I think it's best kept to myself."

"No, it's best said. I've kept little back from you, Wade Bennett. You know more about me than I've allowed any living man to know in five years."

"I suppose what it is is this. We're not so different, you and me. I like to think I won't be wandering forever. I listened to you last night. You kept calling her name in your sleep. Ellen. Talking to her like she was there instead of me."

"I do that sometimes," Billy said, shaking his head. "Don't know why.

For a long time I talked to Mama. But even in the war it was mostly to Ellen."

"There's never been anyone else?"

"I won't say there haven't been other women. I had a Cheyenne girl who kept my cabin in the Rockies for me. But she took a fever and died. That's why I left the place. But there's never been a person to share my heart like Ellen, not even Trav."

"You should've sent for her," Wade said.

"Now how could I have done that? What could I offer her, a gypsy's life? No, she's better off where she is, with her Wise County doctor and that little boy."

"And you?"

"It's not an easy life roaming around, Wade, but there's worse things a man can do with himself. Some men get tied down so hard they never even breathe all the way. Like being drag man on a cattle trail, taking in so much dust you forget what fresh air is."

"Having a home isn't as bad as that,"

Wade said, laughing.

"No, not always. But some men just never were meant to be pinned to the ground."

"I suppose."

While the horses were grazing, Billy and Wade pulled four big catfish out of the water. After enjoying a lunch of fried catfish and wild onions, the two men rode out again onto the plain.

"We're pretty close to a good-sized band of cows, Billy," Wade said. "We'd best ride that way and check 'em. It's not more'n a mile and a quarter, and when we're through, we can head back to the water hole and get our supper."

"You're the boss."

They crossed a series of low hills, chasing an occasional calf back toward the herd. Then they came to the main body, a few hundred shaggy cows and steers huddled around a muddy water hole.

"Everything seems fine here," Wade said.

But Billy motioned for his friend to be

silent. A lone cow a short distance from the others was bawling loudly. Billy rode over and spotted small hoofprints in the sandy ground. Beyond that were other tracks.

"Someone's been here, Wade," Billy said. "Two riders. They spirited away this poor mama cow's baby. She's pretty upset about it by the look of her."

"Would seem so," Wade said. "Two horses, one with heavy hooves. Might be a man and a boy, or a man and a small woman. Not likely outlaws. They'd have taken a steer, maybe several."

"Well, do we find out?"

"That's what the man's paying us for, Billy. You want to lead or follow?"

"That depends on whether you're a tracker. I've followed my share of trails, both man and beast."

"Then I yield to your experience, Major," Wade said.

"I'd just as soon you called me Billy."

"Memories again, huh? Well, can't blame you. God, but she was one pretty woman!"

"Come on," Billy said, nudging Bluebonnet into a trot.

They expected an easy trail to follow, but they found instead that the tracks wound their way over rocky ground and through two creekbeds.

"Seems a lot of trouble to go to, making a hard trail like this," Billy pointed out. "And for a calf. I've got a funny feeling about this, Wade. You might want to keep your rifle handy."

"Know the feeling." Wade sighed. "I've got some icicles running barrel races up my back."

Wade slid his Winchester out of its scabbard and let it rest on his hip. Billy kept his eyes frozen to the trail. Only when a shadow fell across the tracks did he pull up.

"Something up?" Wade asked.

"Probably not. I just have one of those feelings of mine. Let's circle back and go above this ridge."

"You figure somebody's watching us?"

"Well, Wade, these people've been

laying as hard a trail to follow as I've ever seen. Then all of a sudden it's clear as day. I don't take to a man leaving me so good a gift. I start smelling a skunk."

"Then it's the ridge for both of us," Wade said, turning his horse and starting up the steep rise.

The two men had ridden perhaps a hundred yards past the summit of the ridge when something glinted in the sunlight just ahead.

"Steel," Billy announced. "Let's have a closer look."

The two men slid down from their horses and tied the animals to a small mesquite tree. Then they crept on, keeping their eyes alert for any sign of danger. Finally they came upon a low area filled with several heavy boulders. Behind one of the big rocks sat a youthful figure pointing a shotgun toward the road.

"Ambush," Wade whispered.

"Would appear so. Let's slip past him and see what's ahead," Billy suggested.

"Sure," Wade said, nodding his agreement.

Beyond another rise of ground stood a wagon, stripped of its cover. The rear axle was broken, and the back of the wagon rested on two large rocks. A campfire roared in the center of the camp, and a shaggy-haired man and two small boys watched as a woman basted a side of beef that was roasting over the coals.

"We found our calf," Billy whispered. "You stay here and watch the camp. I'll go back and visit our friend with the shotgun."

"Take care, Billy. Shotguns go off easy, you know, and they don't miss much of a man."

"I'll keep that in mind," Billy said.

After leaving Wade, Billy wove through the boulders until he was close enough to smell the young man below him. As Billy approached, he observed the slight build and smooth cheeks of a boy no older than twelve. He crept up slowly, carefully, then grabbed the boy by his hair with one hand while covering his mouth with the other. Before the youthful guard knew what had happened, Billy was sitting on his chest and staring into a pair of wide brown eyes.

"That shotgun would've made a big hole in me if I'd ridden up that trail, eh, boy?" Billy said. "But you have to remember to keep your flanks covered. I'm going to relax my hand now if you promise not to call out. Nod if you swear it."

The boy stared with hate-filled eyes, and Billy drew out his knife.

"I used to camp with the Cheyennes not too far from here, boy," Billy said. "They taught me how you can cut a man's throat so it hardly even bleeds. Then he can't cry out. Now you think it over. You swear to be quiet, or do I start cutting?"

The hate in the boy's eyes was transformed into fear, and he bobbed his head up and down at last.

"Good," Billy said, pulling his hand

back. "I never took to killing youngsters. But then I never took to being shot at from ambush, either. You want to tell me about it?"

"Pa stole a calf," the boy explained. "It was just a small critter, but they said in town how the ranchers hereabouts kill anybody they find camped on the range."

"Oh, so you were going to shoot me because somebody in some two-bit town told you I went gunning after farmers and little boys? Well, you be glad not everything you hear's true. If I was going to shoot you full of holes, I wouldn't be standing over you right now. And before you think about breaking your word and calling out to your pa, you might want to know my partner's got a Winchester rifle aimed at your family right this minute."

Billy stood up and pulled the boy along as he walked back to the horses.

"Where you taking me?"

"Mainly I'm getting my horse. Then we're going to have a talk with that pa of yours who takes to setting ambushes and stealing cattle."

"You won't hurt him?"

"I might just shoot him. Depends on his answers."

"You won't hurt my ma?" the boy asked, trembling. "They say there's a man up here who enjoys shooting women."

"I haven't met up with that one, boy. I've never hurt a woman in my whole life. Or a kid, either, if I could help it. Now come along."

Billy dragged the youngster to where the horses were tied. Then he tied the boy's hands and slung him over the saddle of Wade's pony.

"Sorry to treat you like this, but I don't see another way," Billy said, gagging the boy to prevent any outcry. Then Billy led the horses through the boulders to Wade.

"You did a fair job of that," Wade said, glancing at the squirming boy. "Now it's my turn."

Wade Bennett advanced to the foot of

the camp, keeping his rifle ever ready. The woman dropped her basting brush, and the man fumbled for his musket.

"Before you do anything, mister, you'd best know there's a man in the rocks up there holding a second rifle on you," Wade called out.

To prove it, Billy fired once at the rocks just to the right of the musket.

"You made your point," the man said, holding up his hands. "I won't shoot. We're little threat to you."

The man motioned for his family to join him. The ragged, half-starved boys stood slowly, and two plain-faced girls walked over from behind the wagon.

"We been here close to a week, mister, and we ain't taken but this one little calf," the woman said. "The kids are near starved, and we've no money to pay for a new axle."

"So you decided we wouldn't miss a calf," Wade said. "And the little ambush you arranged for us was really a greeting."

"Where's Bradley?" the woman cried. "Brad?"

"He's where he can't get himself hurt," Billy called to them.

"So, I guess maybe I'll just take a turn around your camp," Wade said, picking up the musket and firing it harmlessly at the sky. Then he removed a pistol from the back of the man's belt, emptied the chambers, and tossed the gun into the fire. When Wade approached the rear of the wagon, the man grew nervous.

"Something here I shouldn't be seeing?" Wade asked, peering inside.

The man stepped back, but Billy fired a warning shot into the sand beside the wagon. The man froze. The children whimpered, and the woman stared at Wade with fierce, angry eyes.

"You got no right, mister," the woman complained.

"I wouldn't be talking rights and wrongs, lady," Wade told her. He reached into the wagon and pulled out the first of several cowhides. "I count six, Billy," Wade announced. "All the brands are the same. Circle M. That's McNally cattle. You been stealing beef for weeks."

"Strays," the man claimed. "This ain't your range."

"Anything north of Texas and south of Kansas is our range," Wade said. "I don't come down here and shoot one of your kids 'cause he might've strayed from your camp. Now you listen real careful to what I got to say. You have two nights to clear out of this country. Get north to Kansas or west to Colorado. But the next time we see you, we'll be shooting at you.

"In these parts," Wade continued, "people have been known to get hurt bad, busted so they can't walk when a night tornado comes through. I'd see to it my family was clear of Mr. McNally's range. If he was here himself, he'd see you hanged for rustling cattle."

"Now you hear me!" the man yelled. "I heard all about your nightriders. They like to shoot ladies and small children in their beds. I'm no woman to be caught with my drawers down. You come on back, and I'll be ready."

"No point in talking to this one, Wade," Billy said, stepping out from the rocks. "I've got nothing personal in this, mister, but something rubs me wrong when a man sets an ambush for me, then has his wife tell lies. Just so you understand what's coming, so you're warned, that's fine. I want my conscience good and clear. I don't like cutting up little boys."

Billy then pulled his Colt and, in a fury of firing, shot off both supports for the barbecue spit, blew a cook pot and a canteen to pieces, then shattered the stock of the discarded musket.

"If you aim to see more of the same, stick around," Billy warned. "Wade here gave you two days, but you didn't seem to care for that. I'll do one better. When I come back tomorrow, you be clear of this place. Understand?"

The man was shaking, and the children whined. The woman stared at the side of beef smoldering in the fire. Billy motioned to Wade, then loosened the ropes that bound young Bradley.

"You remember what I told you, boy," Billy said. "I don't care to warn any man more'n once. A knife does a good clean job of it."

"Yes, sir," the boy said, flying down the hillside to rejoin his family.

"You did one fine job of that," Wade said. "They're not likely to be around much longer."

"You don't know the type," Billy said. "Men like that who leave boys to do their dirty work never learn. I hope he goes. Otherwise I figure we'll be shooting some women and kids near this place."

"Not me," Wade said.

"Not you and me both, Wade. But there won't be a choice. When a boy takes a gun, all the choices up and disappear."

Billy's eyes grew cold and distant, and he urged Bluebonnet into a gallop.

7

A HEAVY silence hung over the camp that Billy and Wade Bennett had made that night. Billy had been different from the instant the first shot had been fired. Wade noticed it and left his friend alone. It was the way of the wandering men who trailed cattle and roamed the open range not to disturb the solitude of a companion.

Billy brooded over how the violence had returned, how that same shadow of gunfire and death always sought him out. In Denver, on the Powder River, even in Dodge City, where he'd lost himself in the card playing and the whiskey. It was always the same. The voice inside him, Ellen's voice, tried to quiet the anger, to hold back the ruthless side of his nature, which made him feared in battle, respected on the plains. But it never brought him love or understanding, least of all by himself.

"I wish you'd given 'em an extra day to get clear, Billy," Wade said as they ate some dried beef bits and cold potatoes Mrs. McNally had sent along. "Did you see the bones sticking out on those little kids? It reminded me of Texas after the war."

"I know." Billy sighed. "But two nights would've given that old man time to set another ambush. This way he's only got time to get on the move."

"Guess you're right," Wade said.

"You know I am. I'll never understand how men like that are the ones to have so many kids at their sides. God, I hate to shoot a man and make five orphans in the process."

That night Billy slept with one eye open. His ears were ever alert for the slightest sound. Noise carried well across the prairie, and no man who wasn't part Indian could approach the camp without attracting Billy's attention.

When morning arrived, Billy mounted

Bluebonnet and prepared to check the camp of the rustler.

"You can stay here if you like, Wade," Billy said. "I don't plan to shoot anybody, and it wouldn't hurt to have our camp guarded."

"All right," Wade said, rolling over into his blankets.

Billy took a circular route back to the squatters' camp, avoiding the rocky southern approach. He picked up wagon tracks bound for Kansas shortly before fording the creek, and he relaxed. When he finally reached the stream, he discovered the wagon bed had been shortened. The bones of the calf remained, so the beef had likely been smoked to feed the children. As he kicked the ashes of the fire to make sure they were cold, a shot rang out from behind him.

The bullet grazed his shoulder, and Billy tumbled to the ground. Bluebonnet shied away, and the shaggy-haired old man emerged from the rocks across the creek.

"Don't look so big now, do you?" the big man called out. "Brad, see if he's got any money on him."

"Pa, he might not be dead," the boy warned.

"Then take my pistol and finish him. Go on, boy. He won't bite."

Billy lay perfectly still, waiting for his moment. When the man lowered his eyes, Billy rolled to the right, drew his Colt, and shot the man once through the head.

"Pa!" the boy screamed, racing to his father's side.

There was nothing to be done, though. Billy had hit what he intended, and no man survived a 44-caliber ball through the head.

"You killed him!" the boy yelled, turning on Billy with a pistol.

"As he thought to've done to me," Billy said, rising to his feet and glancing at the blood trickling down his arm.

"Ma's coming back in another hour. You going to kill her, too?"

"Depends on you," Billy said, pointing

to the pistol. "If you were to raise that piece up and shoot me dead, you could go on stealing cattle for another night or two. If you were the type, that is."

"I never stole anything in my whole life," the boy said, throwing the gun to the ground.

"If your pa could say that, he'd still be alive. Pick up that spade beside the wagon there and help me dig a hole for him."

The boy splashed across the creek, then took the shovel and began to dig. Billy stared at the youthful face, noticing no tears.

"Dig as deep as you can," Billy said. "Then we'll cover it with rocks."

The boy never even glanced up. Billy tore a strip from his shirt and wrapped it tightly around the slice of flesh exposed by the old man's shot. He then dragged the corpse toward the grave. "I'll take a turn," Billy offered, taking the shovel.

"Is that how they always look?" the

boy asked, kneeling beside his father's body. "And the smell?"

"Nothing pretty about death," Billy said. "Your ma'll be here 'fore long. You might want to go off into the rocks and make your peace with him. It's hard to cry in front of women."

"I won't cry!" the boy shouted. "Pa was weak. He lied and cheated at cards. Lost our Missouri bottomland. Then he took to stealing. I'll be stronger."

"There's a time for crying, though," Billy said as he dug. "I cried for my papa, and I was sixteen."

"Then I'm harder than you."

"Maybe," Billy mumbled.

When the grave was dug, Billy helped the boy lower his father into it. Then they filled in the hole with dirt and covered the spot with rocks to ward off wolves.

"It's best I be off before your ma gets back, boy," Billy said. "You might try to make yourself a better man than he was."

He pulled out a twenty-dollar gold

piece and slipped it into the boy's pocket.

"I don't want your money," the boy said, trying to get the coin back out of his tight trousers. "I don't want to clear your conscience."

"If it'd been your pa got himself shot from ambush, then gunned down the man that did it, would you expect his conscience to be bothered?" Billy asked. "I've got no guilt to ease. The gold piece's for you. A man ought to have a little money. And I figure your days of being a boy are gone now."

Without waiting for a reply, Billy climbed onto Bluebonnet's back and rode away. Once again he took the long route back to the camp. He hoped the time alone would help to take the edge off his feelings. It didn't.

When he topped the rise above the water hole where he'd left Wade, Billy was surprised to find a small crowd of mounted men. Wade was missing, but Dunstan and the McNally boys were there. Billy nudged Bluebonnet into a gallop and closed the ground between himself and the others.

"Got some business for you, Starr," Dunstan said when Billy pulled the horse to a stop.

"It's started," Jason McNally said grimly. "A bunch of farmers rode down on us last night and shot up the ranch. They killed my mother and shot Clark Bennett up bad. We followed their tracks to Wolf Canyon. We're ready to get even."

"How do you know they're the right ones?" Billy asked.

"Trailed 'em myself," said a voice from amid the crowd of men. "And I learned to trail camping with my father, a full-blooded Apache."

The speaker stepped forward. He had the appearance of an Indian, and Billy nodded to him.

"I just shot a man myself," Billy said. "He was stealing from the range herd."

"The family young Bennett was talking about," John McNally said.

"We'll tend to them first."

"That's settled," Billy told them.

"Settled?" John asked. "That mean they're all dead?"

"There was only one man," Billy said.

"My ma's lying on the floor dead," John said, fire in his eyes. "I'm not nervous about killing women anymore."

"Then you're a fool!" Billy shouted. "Don't go looking for trouble. Nobody raids a ranch unless he's got men to back the move. We'd best find out what's going on."

"He's right, Johnny," Dunstan said. "We'll go after the others. You all right, Starr?"

"There's blood on your shirt," Jason observed.

"I was grazed by a ball," Billy explained.

"Go on back to the ranch, then," Dunstan said. "Get Buck Davis to tend it. Be ready to ride hard tomorrow. And keep your eyes open tonight."

"Count on it," Billy said, turning his

horse back toward the ranch.

It proved to be a long and difficult ride. Billy reached the big house after sundown. He rode into the clearing in front of the house, calling out that he was a friend. Wade trotted out to greet him, and Mr. McNally, his face showing signs of the strain that had accompanied the death of his wife, stood in the doorway cradling a Winchester.

"Billy, they got hit hard here," Wade said, helping him to the ground. "What happened to you?"

"Oh, that snake of a rustler shot me from ambush this morning. Sent his woman off with the wagon. When I came to look things over, he was ready."

"Did you tell Dunstan? He's got men ready to wipe the plains clean of those farmers."

"I handle my own problems," Billy said. "The shoulder's not bad. I've ridden long and hard on it, though, and it needs to be cleaned and dressed."

"Come on inside the bunkhouse,"

Wade said. "I'll tend it myself. Did you hear about Mrs. McNally?"

"Yeah." Billy sighed. "How's your uncle?"

"Died about three hours ago," Wade said, his lip quivering. "You won't find men feeling sorry for any more little kids, Billy. Clark never hurt a flea. He brought me up from a tadpole after Pa was killed. Somebody'll be paying for this!"

Miguel appeared then, and Billy handed Bluebonnet over to the boy. Wade led the way to the bunkhouse. The wound was cleaned and bound. Soon Billy fell into a deep and untroubled sleep.

In the days that followed, there was a lot of paying for Clark Bennett and Mrs. McNally. The landscape along the Cimarron blazed blood red. Dunstan's horsemen spread a wave of terror for fifty miles in every direction, and the night sky was painted scarlet with burning farms and wagons.

Corn and wheat crops nearly ready for harvest were trampled by horses or put to the torch. A lifetime of accumulated treasures – furniture and livestock, keepsakes and quilts – vanished in a single night raid full of fire and violence.

No one counted the number of men who died during those last weeks of summer. But the flying bullets from Dunstan's Winchesters were blind; they found other marks as well. Grandmothers and small children, wives and daughters, died as well as sons and fathers. It seemed to some that the prairie would run red with blood for years to come.

Billy avoided the raids. His skills weren't required, and he sensed Dunstan didn't entirely trust how he'd behave. Besides, he had no taste for such fighting. His battles had to be personal, face to face. He had to see his enemy, measure him for death. But when Billy recognized the bitterness that had grown in Wade Bennett's eyes, the relish with which young Wade described the hideous fates of farmers burned to death in cellars as the timbers above them collapsed, he mourned for his friend. It was a death of sorts, this love of killing.

Until September the ranchers had it all their way. The numbers of the farmers and settlers lessened dramatically. It was hard to find a single field growing anything but tall blue stem grasses and sagebrush.

It changed one morning when a wagon pulled into the ranch proper carrying the body of Art Danby. Danby had been feared and respected throughout the Southwest. One month he'd killed half a dozen young men who'd come one by one to try their hand against the legendary fastest gun in the Cimarron.

"Danby's dead," Miguel whispered to Billy. "They got him in the wagon, sẽnor. He got a hole under his left eye. A big hole."

Billy didn't bother to look. He'd seen death in all its varieties.

"The man who did this," Dunstan said to the men on the wagon. "What was his name?"

"Parker," Hank Jordan said. "I heard he was down from Santa Fe. It's for certain somebody brought him in."

"How fast is he?" Dunstan asked.

"Fast enough," Hank said. "I never seen hands that quick. And Mike, he said he's waiting in town for you. Said you'd best come see him or start packing. He kind of hinted he was expecting other company from Santa Fe."

"Someone's called in help," Dunstan said. "We've got a full-fledged range war working now."

In the hours following Danby's death, there was a lot of practising going on down past the corrals. Young John McNally boasted to everyone in sight about how he'd take care of Danby's killer personally. But it was Wade Bennett who chose to take the wagon back into Cimarron City for supplies.

"He'll kill you, Wade," Billy warned.

"Does it matter?" Wade asked. "I'm dead anyway. I've smelled the killing too often. I can't go back."

"You understand what it's like now," Billy said, nodding. "I'll go with you."

"You sure?" Wade asked.

"Sure as ever I am."

Billy sent Miguel to tell Dunstan they were leaving. Then the two Texans got aboard the wagon and set off for town.

8

BILLY and Wade got no more than a mile from the ranch when they heard the sound of hooves pounding the road behind them. Wade pulled the wagon to a stop, and moments later Dunstan appeared.

"You boys don't seriously think you're going to town, do you?" Dunstan asked.

"That was the idea," Wade said. "I heard there was a man looking for someone there."

"And you were going to oblige him, were you?" Dunstan said, shaking his head. "I didn't keep you here all winter, Bennett, to have you gunned down before trailing the herd to market. And you, Starr, I've got big plans for you."

"Don't start in with me, Dunstan," Billy said. "You brought me out here for one thing: to use my gun. So that's what I plan to do."

"That's right," Dunstan said. "And we'll kill that man dead enough when the time comes. But it's best done my way. You'll get to a point where you can ride into town and shoot a man down, but you're not there yet. You're good, Starr. I saw that in Dodge. But you still have to have a reason to draw down on a man, and that slows the hand. We do this my way."

Billy started to argue, but a glance at Dunstan's hard jaw stopped him. He suddenly felt like an apprentice standing before the old master, Dunstan.

"Now, Bennett, you ride on to town. You find out all you can about this new man, this Parker. But you keep your guns in the wagon, you hear me?"

"I hear you," Wade said, the bitterness in his voice obvious. "I'm supposed to snake around, hide my face from the bad men, be another Miguel. Well, I'm no kid."

"A man does his fighting when and where it counts, Bennett," Dunstan explained. "You won't do anything for Clark by getting yourself shot to pieces. Danby was the best I've ever seen. Only two men could've taken him. Texas Bob Smith and maybe Luke Hall. Smith would never lend his pistol to farmers, so this Parker must be Hall."

"Or somebody you don't know, like me," Billy said.

"Not likely," Dunstan told them. "Be a real rare day when two fast men came out of the mountains. And I expect you've seen some fighting before, Starr. Down Texas way, maybe?"

Billy's eyes betrayed the truth, and Dunstan smiled.

"Now get yourself to town, Bennett," Dunstan commanded. "And remember what I said. A smart snake lives a long time, you know."

Billy watched with mixed feelings as his friend headed toward Cimarron City alone.

"I'm going along," Billy suddenly told Dunstan.

"All you'll do is get the both of you

killed," Dunstan told him. "If it's Hall, he's got no interest in running up a score. He hasn't shot many, but the ones he's nailed were the best. And they were dead before they hit the ground."

"Then Wade's safe?"

"From Hall. My guess is he'll only pass on a message. They want me, Starr."

"Why you?" Billy asked.

"You never fought a range war before. It's a simple kind of a thing, really. Both sides hire soldiers, just like in a war. You can kill off a fast gun, shoot a dozen soldiers, but if you find out who the top man is and cut him down, you win the war. That's the whole trouble with this mess we've gotten ourselves into. I don't know who's doing the hiring, who's behind this thing. Until I do, we just hold our ground, bait them out."

"We can take this Parker or Hall or whatever his name is."

"We will take him before he gets us. Before he brings in a bunch of his buddies from Santa Fe. Gunmen, the good ones, have a survival instinct. They hear there's a fast hand around, they clear out until they find someone to challenge him."

"That's what you're doing," Billy said.

"And what they did when Danby was around."

"So, what do we do now?"

"Learn," Dunstan said.

It was hard for Billy to return to the ranch with Dunstan, but he did. When Wade came back with the supplies and the latest news that afternoon, Billy was very relieved.

"I figure you're right about Parker, Mike," Wade told Dunstan. "He wears twin Colts and carries a Winchester. He's got a belt buckle with a big *H* on it, too."

"It's Hall, all right," Dunstan said. "He's got wavy red hair, a scar on his left temple. He has a big gold tooth in the front of his mouth."

"That's the man," Wade agreed. "But

that's not all. He talks some. It appears he's killed twelve men."

"Twelve?" Dunstan said, smiling. "Well, there's a piece of luck. Next one makes thirteen. Hall's superstitious. I'll bet he's nervous as a blue tick hound."

"Sam down at the livery says Parker keeps an extra-sharp lookout at night."

"Then he's liable to be a little short on sleep. Good," Dunstan said, smiling in his wicked sort of way.

"Tell the rest, Wade," Billy urged.

"While I was there, freight wagons were bringing in lumber. Whole loads of the stuff. Enough for a school and a church, Mike. And more. There's talk of handing Parker a badge."

"Makes no sense," Dunstan said. "I can see what the town's up to; trying to build up support for a territorial marshal. But Hall needs no badge. All the authority he needs comes with that pair of revolvers on his hips."

"I saw something else, Mike," Wade said. "There's a new man at the hotel.

He's tall and speaks with a Yankee accent. Used to be some sort of judge."

"Well, now, that straightens out who's behind all this, doesn't it?" Dunstan said. "The judge staying in town?"

"Left when he heard I was there," Wade told them. "In a bit of a hurry, too, so I heard."

"Then we take care of Mr. Hall first and afterward locate the judge. Starr," Dunstan said, turning to Billy, "best you have some target practice before that. There's other things to learn, too. We start for the range early tomorrow."

Billy's lessons were exhausting. Dunstan had him shooting. Shooting and shooting and shooting. With both hands.

"A man can get himself shot in the hand, Starr," Dunstan explained. "Sometimes before the job's done."

Billy learned to fire from every angle, at every time of day or night.

"Know you can shoot, Starr," Dunstan said when Billy complained. "But you can be faster. And there's a flaw in your draw. You glance at your foot a second. You got to do the drawing by reflex. A good gunman would move when you look down. You end up missing your first shot. And with Hall you don't get a second one."

So Billy practiced until he could draw and shoot with his eyes closed, in the middle of the night, or facing the sun. When they finished, Dunstan smiled.

"You're as good as they come with your hands, Starr," the older man announced. "But I guess those eyes of yours will always tell how good you'll be in a fight."

"What've my eyes got to do with it?" Billy asked.

"Well, when they get all full of fury like that time in Dodge, I figure you could take Texas Bob, Hall, and Danby all at one time. But when they're soft and easygoing, like now, you're more a danger to yourself than anybody else."

"There's little soft about me, Dunstan," Billy declared.

"Make it Mike. You ought to call a man by his first name when he knows you inside out like I do. Remember that. Sometimes it keeps a man in line to know there's somebody that knows him better'n he knows himself."

"Don't be too confident of that, Dunstan."

"Call me Mike."

"All right, Mike," Billy said, glaring at the older man. "Don't get to feeling you know me too well. You know somebody named Billy Starr. I've been a lot of different men, though, and I'll be others before I'm through. Know something else, too. I don't like you very much."

"That's all right, Starr," Dunstan said, smiling. "I like you just fine."

Certainly it seemed that way. Dunstan sent for a new outfit for the man he'd dubbed Starr. Included were a cotton shirt and trousers, white as new-fallen snow; a leather vest with an *S* stamped on each pocket; high brown boots; and a broad-brimmed white hat.

"Fit to be stuffed," Wade observed when Billy tried the outfit on for size.

"I like my old hat better," Billy said, removing the new one.

"You'd better leave that gray one in the bunkhouse for a time. I saw some Texas boys in town this morning. I recognized one as an old friend of your brother's."

Billy led Wade off to one side of the room.

"You sure?" Billy whispered.

"I recall him well enough. He was the carpetbagging Yank judge that grabbed the Cobbs' place down on the Brazos from them."

"I hope he's out of town when I meet Hall," Billy said. "Talk to the Texans. See if any of them are from Palo Pinto County."

"It's important to you, isn't it?"

"Yes. And Wade, see to it Dunstan doesn't hear about this."

"He scares you, doesn't he?"

"He'd scare the devil. The man's got no soul. I never knew a man before to have no loyalties at all."

"That's Dunstan."

Another week passed, and still Billy stayed at the ranch. All the while Dunstan worked on the nerves of Luke Hall. More than one passing stranger commented about how thirteen was clearly an unlucky number. Others told stories of how this or that proved to be bad luck. They would then arrange for that very calamity to befall Luke Hall.

It was a Friday morning when Billy finally rode into Cimarron City to settle things. Wade met him and Dunstan at the edge of town with the news that the mysterious judge had ridden out of town to pass the day with his wife. Billy and Dunstan then went directly to the hotel.

"Remember, don't call him out, Starr," Dunstan instructed. "Let him come to you."

"I know what to do," Billy said coldly. "We've practiced it often enough."

"Then don't make any mistakes. I'm

not accustomed to depending on people, Starr. You fail to kill this man, I'm dead, too."

"Keep in mind that failing means I go down myself," Billy said, frowning. "I wouldn't care to do that."

The hotel was the sole structure in town with a second floor. The upstairs rooms were for travelers, of which there were few. Downstairs, there was a parlor where gentlemen might play cards. There were few gentlemen in Cimarron City, though. Behind the parlor was a hall lined with rooms that could be rented to various ladies who chose to entertain personal guests for the evening.

Still, all in all, the hotel was the most respectable of the town's buildings, except perhaps for the small mercantile run by Miss Jessica Hart. Miss Hart's father, Herbert, had built the place, but an unfortunate accident while playing blackjack had led to his early departure from the world. The young woman now carried on the business with the aid of a younger brother.

"Good morning, Miss Hart," Dunstan said to the woman as they met on the walk in front of the hotel.

"Mr. Dunstan," Miss Hart said, nodding slightly.

"Have you met Mr. Starr?" Dunstan asked.

"Sir, I have not," the young woman said, smiling at Billy.

"My pleasure, ma'am," Billy said, nudging Dunstan to move along.

"Beg your pardon, ma'am, but we've an appointment to keep," Dunstan explained.

"Certainly," Miss Hart told them.

As they walked past, Billy heard her whisper "Devil take you" to Dunstan. It brought a smile to his lips.

It was to be the last smile for a time. Luke Hall sat at his usual table in the parlor, playing cards with a woman named Moore from Ohio and her brother. Billy walked to the table and bowed.

"Can you use a fourth?" he asked.

"If you can afford our game," the man from Ohio said.

"Will three hundred dollars buy me a seat?" Billy asked.

"Yes, of course," the woman said.

Billy played cautiously. The innocent-looking woman dealt seconds, and her brother had more than one ace up his lace-covered cuff. Hall played honest, resting his cold steel revolvers beside his hands atop the table. Billy observed that the Ohio couple kept Hall's losses within modest bounds.

Billy, on the other hand, they would cheat without mercy. He played his cards tight and with a certain unpredictability that disrupted their cheating. Three aces didn't beat a full house, even when two of them were drawn from a sleeve. And Billy cut the deck effectively, often disturbing a carefully prepared round.

"Tell me, son, have we met before?" Hall asked Billy as the game continued. "You play well enough to have crossed my path."

"Doubt it, Mr. Parker," Billy said. "Somebody told me you spend most of your time in New Orleans."

"Santa Fe," Hall said, breathing easier. "Ever been there?"

"No. I was in Denver a year or so back. But I've mainly kept to the high Rockies, up in Shoshoni country."

"Running with Indians, huh?" Hall asked.

"Sometimes," Billy admitted.

"Never took to having Indian-lovers at my table," Hall said, laughing. "I ever tell you how I cut open three runt kids in a Cheyenne village up on Sand Creek?"

"Dear Lord," said Miss Moore, turning a shade of green.

"It appears this lady has a weak stomach," Billy said, forcing a smile to his face. "Me, I've seen all sorts of things in my time."

"Like maybe a gunfight or two?" Hall asked.

"Could be," Billy said.

"If you'll excuse us, sirs, I believe

we'd best be leaving," Miss Moore announced.

"Fine with me," Hall said. "But leave the cash. I don't take kindly to being cheated at cards."

Hall grabbed his pistols and pointed them at the two Ohioans. Both dropped their winnings on the table and beat a hasty retreat.

"Now, why don't you just follow them along, son?" Hall asked Billy, swinging the pistols over at him.

"Not likely. Not with two hundred dollars of my money on this table," Billy said, the hardness coming to his eyes.

"Only another cheat wouldn't call their little game," Hall said.

"I don't have to cheat. And it was your game. When I sit at a stranger's table, I accept the risks. It's hardly a safe undertaking to challenge a game when two Colts rest on the table."

"Well, that is a point," Hall said, laughing. "But I aim to keep the money."

"There's a more gentlemanly way to settle the issue," Billy said. "One hand, one draw. You deal and I'll cut. Either man cheats, we settle it outside."

"I don't have to cheat either, my young friend," Hall said, shuffling the cards. "I started playing poker before I could talk. And Lady Luck walks at my side."

The cards were dealt, and the money was stacked in the center of the table. The game attracted a crowd as the two players held their cards against their chests and exchanged cold, hard looks.

Billy gazed at his cards. He felt his insides quake. A pair of fours. Billy took three new cards. Hall announced he needed but one, and that improved Billy's state of mind not a bit. But among the three new cards were two beautiful black jacks.

"Well, did you by chance pick up your third of a kind?" Hall asked. "If you'll notice, I did not draw my needed nine." The man spread out four-fifths of a straight flush. "But

I did pair up my ten," he added, placing a ten of clubs alongside the ten of hearts.

"As a matter of fact, I didn't," Billy said, revealing the two fours. "But I did draw a fine pair of jacks."

"Two pairs beat one," someone behind the table announced.

Billy reached for the money, but Hall stood up, frowning.

"Not likely," Hall said. "Win or lose, that cash isn't leaving the table."

"So, it's come to this, has it?" Billy asked.

"You knew it would," Hall said. "I saw you earlier with Dunstan. So now we'll take care of business."

Billy backed away from the table, spreading his hands wide so that his fingers could flirt with the handle of his pistol. The spectators scrambled to get out of the way.

"What do they call you?" Hall asked.

"Starr," Billy said coldly.

"Well, Starr, let's get on with it."

"Gentlemen, please," pleaded Mr.

Brown, the hotel owner. "Not in my hotel."

"We won't shoot it up much," Hall said, laughing. "Fact is, I don't figure a ball would get through either of our tough old hides A little blood maybe, but that washes off a rug in time."

"Please don't," someone begged from the other side of the room.

Billy paid no attention. His eyes were frozen on the tall man's hands. Hall waited what seemed an eternity to make a move. Remember what Dunstan taught you, Billy, he told himself. Keep your eyes belt-high. And shoot to kill.

For the first time there was thinking to it. Always before, Billy's instincts had taken over. The killing had been a thing done without feeling, strangely detached from the rest of his world. Now it was confronting him, hammering at his conscience.

"Anytime, Starr," Hall said.

Suddenly Billy's mind cleared. His hands relaxed, and the sweat vanished from his palms. As Hall finally reached for his revolvers, Billy's right hand went into motion. As if frozen in time, Billy watched the other man's Colts draw level, watched his fingers press the triggers. But his own quicker hand had already fired, and Hall's chest exploded. Blood spattered the table, the rug, and Hall's pistols fired into the floor.

"My God!" someone screamed.

"He's dead," pronounced a voice that Billy recognized from another place, another time.

Turning, Billy viewed the face of a man dressed in a black suit. It was the judge, the Ohio Yank who'd nearly stolen the ranch Billy's father had carved out of the wilderness.

"You!" the judge shouted, drawing back. His eyes bore traces of surprise mixed with terror.

Judge Fulton's hand reached inside his coat, and a second shot rang out. Billy watched the eyes of his old enemy freeze. The judge dropped first to his knees, then toppled to the floor face first. Turning, Billy saw the smoking pistol Dunstan was holding.

"You all saw it!" Dunstan said, pointing at the dead man. "He was going for his gun."

The others stared at the judge's widow.

"He never carried a gun," the woman said, weeping.

"How was I to know?" Dunstan asked.

"Right, Mike," someone said, slapping Dunstan on the back.

"Whatever you say, Mike," another commented.

The crowd began nodding and patting Billy on the back. But Billy had no time for any of them. He collected the money from the table and wove his way through the throng of people to the street. Only fresh air could keep him from vomiting. And nothing would chase away the smell of death from his hands.

9

BILLY left town without uttering a word. For a long time he wandered the low hills and creek bottoms that marked the Cimarron landscape. From time to time he passed clusters of grazing cattle and small herds of wild horses. And there were, of course, the sod houses of the few remaining farmers.

Always the past comes back to you, Billy thought as he rode. No matter how far you run, how often you move around, some face, some shadow of that past returns.

Billy wondered if Dunstan realized what a favor he had done him by silencing the judge. Billy felt no pangs of conscience for having contributed to that man's death. Judge Fulton was a liar, a cheat, and a thief. It was fitting that he should die at the hands of a man like Dunstan, a man not unlike himself.

Billy made a camp on a rise of ground a mile or so from the McNally ranch buildings. He felt a strong need to be alone that night. Killing always drove him either to someone or away from everyone. It was no different this time.

The killing itself had been, though. He'd shot men before, two or three in a day during the war. But it had never been planned or calculated to the last detail as had the death of Luke Hall. This was a killing engineered like a barn raising, put together in pieces like one of his mama's old cut-up puzzles. Billy had once imagined it would be like doing battle against a knight, akin to one of the stories in the book about King Arthur he'd read as a wide-eyed twelve-year-old. But there had been no valor, no hint of chivalry. It had been cold, cruel, just as murder always was.

Shiloh came back to him, that terrible rainy night after the first day's fighting. The cold and the wetness had penetrated his thin coat, and he'd been shaking from head to toe. It was the night he'd watched his father's eyes close for a final time, when once and for all he'd stood alone facing a hostile world.

Billy felt the same chill now. It was close to ninety degrees, and there wasn't a trace of wind or a cloud to be found in the sky overhead. The cold that gripped him came from inside. It was from the killing, from the casual way he'd gone about ending a human life that morning. And it was from the suddenness of death, the finality of Hall's silent, frozen eyes.

You rode to town today to kill a man, Billy told himself. You've done some things in your time, but always after being pushed around or backed into a corner. You never sold your soul to do the devil's bidding before.

It was a terrifying thought. Long before, Billy had given up hope of living the life he'd dreamed of as a boy. Since turning away from the Texas ranch of his birth, he'd accepted the life and fate of a wayfarer. But somehow there'd always been an inner dream, a hope of something better in the next world. Now that was gone, too.

Billy spread out his horse blanket and tried to find some rest. But his eyes would not close; his conscience would not be still. He kept staring at the sky, hoping some soothing voice would come down to him, as it had on the high cliffs above the Brazos and again amid the tall peaks of the Rockies. The voice did not come, though.

Wade Bennett finally found Billy the following morning. The young man from Waco walked slowly into Billy's camp, softly whistling an old cattle tune. Billy looked up, recognized Wade, and nodded.

"Figured you might take to the hills," Wade whispered. "Comes of growing up around Indians, I expect."

"Maybe," Billy said. "Mainly it's the killing."

"You did it clean enough. I didn't think anything bothered you."

"That's the trouble," Billy said, looking away. "It was so simple. I didn't even blink."

"You can't start feeling sorry about killing a man like Hall, not one who'd murder Clark and poor Mrs. McNally."

"What kind of man should I be sorry for killing, Wade? I didn't mourn killing the old man down by the creek. I had no regrets about the two cowboys back in Dodge."

"Look, he ran the same risk you did," Wade pointed out. "He took his guns to town, accepted gold for killing Danby. Others, too. You didn't shoot him down in a dark alley or catch him unarmed, his wife at his side, like Dunstan did that judge. You met him face to face."

"That judge recognized me." Billy sighed.

"I heard. Old Dunstan did the whole of Texas a favor by gunning down that man. Glad his woman had tears for him. Nobody else will."

"Kept my secret quiet."

"Billy, why don't you go back now?"

Wade asked sitting on the ground beside his friend. "With the carpetbaggers gone, maybe your brother will welcome you home."

"I told you," Billy said sadly. "There's no going back for me, not now, not ever. I've been thinking about heading for the mountains, though. Everything seems simpler in the high country. I've never been to California. Maybe I can make a clean start of it there."

"Can't run away forever," Wade said. "What happened yesterday morning was a simple matter of self-defense. You shot Hall. He'd have killed you if he'd had the chance. That's certain."

"I never figured to stay here forever."

"I guess that's true enough. Seems kind of stupid to me to stay through the hard times, though, just to ride off into the mountains for winter."

"It'd be easier for two, Wade."

"What good would I be in the mountains? I'm a fair man with cattle. I know that. No, I'll stick to the herds."

They talked more as the morning

brightened. Then Billy saddled his horse and followed Wade back to the ranch.

"Been wondering when you'd come in, Starr," Dunstan said when Billy climbed down from his horse in front of the bunkhouse. "Got some money for you."

"Money?" Billy asked.

"Twenty for this last week, and another hundred as a bonus."

"Bonus?"

"Fifty for each man killed. If it was up to me, I'd have given you double for Hall, triple even. But McNally's gotten tightfisted all of a sudden."

"I didn't shoot them for the money," Billy said angrily.

"Sure you did," Dunstan told him. "You might tell yourself something different, but money entered into it. Here."

Dunstan dropped six twenty-dollar gold pieces into Billy's hand. Billy stuffed the coins in his pocket, then turned away to help Wade tend the horses. The other hands offered congratulations, but Billy accepted them with a stern and lifeless face.

A spell of peace fell over the land along the Cimarron for weeks following the deaths of Hall and Judge Fulton. The church and the school were finished, but few people were seen inside the simple wooden structures. The ground floor of the hotel was still crowded, and the singing and card playing from the three saloons kept up through the wee hours of the mornings.

The McNally crew was busy trailing cattle to market. Weeks spent on the dusty trail to the railhead at Abilene came as a relief to Billy. The work left him weary at day's end, and for a time the shadows of his past were set aside.

Those farmers who chose to stay that autumn made their homes close to town. They broke the sod away from the pastures grazed by McNally herds. And aside from walking or riding in wagons to attend school, no children were to be seen unless guarded by at least one man with a shotgun.

"This war's about done with," Dunstan remarked over a Saturday-night barbecue. "Cut off the head, huh, Starr? Chop down the leader and the rest of the sheep scatter for cover."

It appeared to be all too true. The farmers who remained lacked anything resembling unity of purpose. No more gunmen arrived in town to test the hand of Billy Starr. And the mere mention of that name sent nightmares through the minds of the children sleeping in the loft of a barn or on the cold dirt floor of a soddy.

That winter proved cold even for the Cimarron country. Deep snowdrifts blew across the prairie in early January, and farmers and ranchers alike were most concerned with staying warm and keeping their stock from freezing.

Spring restored life to the plains, though. Word came that the Texas cattle herds would soon be crossing the Llano, bound for markets in Dodge City. Dunstan sent his riders out across the range once more, spreading terror and reminding the farmers who held dominion over the Cimarron plain.

Billy again found himself paired with Wade Bennett, assigned to patrol an isolated region of gullies and boulders along the southern bank of the river. No one on the ranch had spotted a farmer or even a maverick steer anywhere near there. The only water was that in the river, and the ground was bone hard, a nightmare for anyone hoping to break the earth with a plow.

There was a lot of mumbling around the ranch when Billy saddled his horse and prepared to head for the river.

"You don't send your top-gun hand to Kansas," one of the men complained. "There'll be trouble 'cause of this."

"Can't let up on them farmers," another added.

But as Billy and Wade set out across the barren landscape, Dunstan only smiled.

He's the devil, Billy thought to himself, glancing back at the man's coal-black eyes. He can look right through a man's head and read his soul.

"What's on your mind, Billy?" Wade asked.

"I was just thinking about Dunstan," Billy said. "He's a strange man, sending us out here away from everything. And just when I'd about decided to pack up and head for Colorado."

"He knew, Billy," Wade said. "You said something to Miguel about going to Denver. Miguel, he tells old Mike anything that might earn him an extra dollar. I'll tell you, though, the boys are none too happy about it."

"Let 'em be unhappy," Billy grumbled. "I don't owe them anything."

"Haven't you found your peace yet?" Wade asked, shaking his head. "It's been close to six months. You know, there's been no killing around here in all that time. By anybody. That's on account of you, Billy."

"Even if that was true, it's hardly a credit to say I did something right by not killing anybody for half a year."

Wade laughed for a minute.

"Around here, six months with no dead bodies lying around is close to a miracle," Wade said, kicking his horse into a trot. "And if you don't feel any peace, well, I'm sorry for you. You've brought some to the rest of us."

Billy spent a pleasant six weeks riding the open range with Wade Bennett. There was time for fishing, hard riding, even hunting a pair of buffalo from a small herd down from Kansas.

"You know, Billy," Wade said, "I been all my life in Texas and the plains country. I shot my first deer before I could shave. But this is the first time I ever shot a buff. It's a different kind of thing, a bit like trying to rope thunder."

"I guess," Billy said. "I do it with a sadness in my heart. Used to be the prairie was black with the big woolies. Nowadays it's rare to spot a single one."

"Still, it's something to tell your

grandkids, how you shot yourself a buff down on the Cimarron."

"That what you want out of life, Wade? Grandkids?"

"Well, I was thinking how maybe when I save enough money, I'd go back to McLennan County, buy me a piece of good land for corn and a wide stretch for cattle. They'll have the rails through to Waco in five years, it's said. Run cattle and raise kids. Not a bad life for a Texas boy."

"Calm sort of life," Billy noted.

"You live longer that way," Wade said, laughing. "No stampedes or dry gulchers. No Art Danbys and Luke Halls around. Just Texas rangers and law and order."

"Lots of fences down there," Billy said. "Never took much to fences."

"Me neither," Wade said, "but working for your own self wouldn't be all that bad."

"Oh, there's always somebody, Wade. Some judge like Fulton. Some local man with ambition. There's always men around with a will to own you."

"I suppose."

"You're lucky, though, Wade. Right now a man can still lose himself, find a place in the high country or out here on the range with nobody else around. If he's strong enough to get by on his own, that is."

But Billy knew that no matter how strong a man was, he couldn't run far enough to escape his past. And it wasn't something that could be erased, either, not even with six weeks of hunting buffalo and sharing the range with Wade Bennett.

10

THE passing of March brought a change to the Cimarron. Word came that the Texas herds would be moving across the Llano in late spring, and the men at the McNally ranch sprang into action. For Billy and Wade it meant leaving the peace of the river to return to the long hours and hard work of a ranch hand.

In the beginning the work was to Billy's liking. A herd of wild mustangs had wandered onto the range, and Billy and Wade led three other hands in search of the horses. The animals were small, powerful ponies well suited to a cattleman's craft. They were led by a tall white stallion that would have done justice to an army general.

Billy had always possessed an eye for such horses. Old Thunder, the mount that had brought him through the final days of the war and back to Texas, was such a horse. Comanche had been taken from the freedom of the range and gentled. Now Billy found himself longing to have the great white stallion.

"Cloud Dancer," Billy mumbled as they watched the horse from a distant ridge. "I remember a Cheyenne riding a horse like that. Young, strong, with a will to match the stars."

But even a smart horse was no match for a man. A makeshift corral was built to enclose a small canyon, and the riders set out to drive the horses into it.

Billy took the left, Wade the right, and the others ran the ponies hard from behind. The proud white tried to turn in one direction, then another. Now and then a horse broke away and made good its escape, but Billy and Wade steered the stallion on toward the canyon.

It was not an easy thing to do. The horse was more than strong. It was brave as well, and it fought to break out from the encircling horsemen. The animal had run long and hard, though, and there was not enough power left in its being to elude forever the host of determined pursuers.

Billy watched the horse, smiling with admiration at the beast. The stamina, the power, and the grace of the stallion built a fire inside him. There was a lust for life in that horse. Even as its eyes burned red with fatigue, it refused to yield. Still it tried its tricks, battled the inevitable.

By the time they closed on the canyon, the great white horse had spent its energy. The stallion found it impossible to halt its stampeding companions. The leader, along with the other mustangs, was swept along through the open gate of the corral. As the rails were slid into place to block the herd's escape, the cowboys cheered.

"Seems a shame somehow to rob such a horse of his freedom." Billy sighed as the dust settled.

"He's a horse," Wade told him. "I've seen your eyes. You mean to gentle him so that he'll carry you into the clouds."

Billy looked on as the other animals stomped their hooves and stared at the steep walls of the canyon, at the high rails of the fence, at the men who had trapped them.

"Tomorrow we start breaking them to saddle," one of the others said. "Mike'll be happy, not to mention Mr. McNally. Good horseflesh'll bring top dollar when them Texans get up here. Must be a hundred horses at least. And that white, well, he's worth a thousand dollars easy."

"He's mine," Billy said quietly.

"Right, Starr," the man said. "You earned him. God, but he's a live one. You going to geld him? That usually takes the rambler out of 'em."

"What good's a horse without spirit?" Billy asked.

"Wade tells me that black you ride is a range stallion," another of the men said.

"Was," Billy told them. "He runs with the wind, too, but a man needs more than one runner."

"True enough," the third man said. "I been on the run before. Found myself close to a rope for shooting a Kansas farmer. Nearly got hanged for lack of a fresh horse."

The men continued to converse about horses for a time. Then the herd stirred, and Billy rose to his feet, Winchester in hand.

"Billy, they're just restless," Wade said.

"Might be a wolf," Billy whispered. "I'll tend to it."

Billy made his way to the corral. There, twenty yards away, stood the great white stallion, pawing the ground and breathing hard.

"It's all right, Cloud Dancer," Billy called to the animal. "Soon enough you'll get to know me. I won't rob you of your spirit."

The stallion dipped its head and screamed into the night. Then it turned to the others. It seemed to Billy that it had understood.

But it was not so. Billy heard the horses stomping and turned in time to spot the white horse start up the wall of the canyon.

"No horse climbs the wall of a canyon!" Billy shouted. "You'll break your legs!" It was like pleading with the sky for rain.

"Wade!" Billy called to his friend.

"Coming," Wade cried, grabbing his rifle and racing to Billy's side.

"Look up there," Billy said, pointing to where the horse was gingerly making its way up the hillside.

"He's trying to get away," Wade said. "No horse can climb a canyon wall, though. Not even a mule could make it up that slope."

"He knows that," Billy said, sadly observing the stallion's progress. "He knows there's no chance, but he's going anyway. He'd rather die than be penned up."

"Don't be stupid. A horse doesn't think like that. He's just searching for a way out."

"No, he's making his last break."

The two friends leaned on the rails of the corral and watched the horse climb higher. Then the ground beneath its hooves gave way and the stallion fell.

It wasn't a quick and painless fall. It was a rolling, sliding, scraping kind of tumble, the type that strips away the flesh of a man or beast, busts his bones, and torments his soul. In the end the great white horse got to its knees and whinnied. Blood stained its mouth, and its cries were unearthly. Billy shivered.

Billy raised his Winchester slowly.

"You can't hit anything from here," Wade said. "Not in this light."

Billy stared through the sights at the horse. It was growing dark, but the mane of the white horse stood out from the darkness like a beacon.

"Billy, don't," Wade pleaded. "We can do this in the morning."

"Can't you hear him?" Billy asked, his eyes red. "He's in pain. An animal like that, one with the heart to try, shouldn't be forced to endure that kind of pain."

Billy cocked the rifle, then aimed. He squeezed the trigger, and the terrible whinnying ceased. The other horses stirred, and the echo of the shot rang through the canyon like some cry from the underworld.

"You really think he knew what would happen?" Wade asked, prying Billy's fingers from the Winchester and setting the gun down. "You think he couldn't stand the notion of being penned up?"

"You can't clip an eagle's wings," Billy said. "Not and call him an eagle anymore."

"Guess not," Wade said, frowning.

It took the better part of a week to get the horses under control, and another week to get the first of them gentled. Wade and Billy did it the hard way. The others used whips and ropes and spurs. But when it was over, Billy and his friend had mounts that could outrun the wind. The other ponies were adequate and nothing more.

Billy was haunted by the death of the white stallion. He often found his thoughts drifting back to the proud horse that had refused to yield.

Stubborn mustang! Billy thought. Bucking the natural order of things, defying fate. And all the while Billy admired the creature, even in its dying agonies.

It was late April when their work was interrupted by the arrival of young Jason McNally.

"We've got trouble in town, Starr," the young man told Billy. "Jack Sanford got himself shot. Mike wants you to come in tomorrow and handle it."

"I'll be in when we finish gentling the horses," Billy said. "You tell Dunstan."

"That's not why we keep you around," Jason said angrily. "You're our top gun. Everybody knows that."

"Tell Dunstan to attend to it himself,"

Billy said. "I'm doing no more killing for him."

"Then you'd best pack your gear!" Jason shouted. "We sure don't plan on paying any cowboys twenty dollars a week!"

"Fair enough," Billy said, stalking off to collect his gear.

"Hold on, Starr," Harry Gilbert pleaded. "Young McNally there's got a big mouth. I'll ride in with Jason and talk to Dunstan, tell him you've got work to finish."

"Mike won't like that," Jason said.

"Well, that flat breaks my heart," Billy said, a faint smile crossing his lips. "You tell him."

"So, you're through with the killing, huh?" Wade asked as Jason rode off.

"I'm trying," Billy explained. "That wasn't hard to say."

"It'll be harder to do. You don't know Dunstan as well as I do. He's a hard man to turn down. Doesn't give up."

"I took him for that sort. But I've

got close to a thousand dollars in my saddlebags. Gambling money and wages. I can live a long time on that much money."

"It's enough to start that place I was telling you about, Billy," Wade said. "We could go partners, you know."

"Not in Texas." Billy sighed.

"There's land in Colorado. Good range that can be had cheap. How about that?"

"Interesting thought," Billy said, leaning against a large boulder. "I've got a sister somewhere in Colorado."

"We could find a couple of fine young farm girls and build a big wooden house. Run cattle and horses."

"And kids?" Billy asked.

"Damned right," Wade said, laughing. "A hundred at least. Cheaper'n hiring hands."

The two of them laughed for a moment. Then they heard a horse galloping up. The hands of all five men reached for their rifles, but Wade broke out laughing.

"It's just the McNally kid," he said. "Come back with Dunstan's answer."

The men relaxed. If Billy's thinking had been straighter, he would have realized that young Jason hadn't been gone long enough to pass a message on to anyone. As the boy dove from his horse, shots rang out from the rocks all around them.

"I tried to warn you!" Jason shouted, rolling over beside Billy. "Must be twenty of 'em. Riders I never seen before."

"Spread out," Billy said, motioning to his companions to fall back to the scattered boulders that marked the entrance to the canyon. "Stay down!"

"My God!" old Jake Fowler cried out, staring at the two bodies that had fallen beside him. "They got the others, Starr!"

The rifles barked again, and old Jake fell, his chest blown apart.

"What do we do now?" Wade asked, crawling over beside Billy. Wade swung his Winchester toward the shadows slipping in and out of the distant rocks.

"What else?" Billy asked, his eyes full of violence again. "We fight back."

11

BILLY snaked his way through the rocks until he arrived at a small gully. The rocks provided natural cover. It was the perfect place to make a stand. Bracing himself against a boulder, he loaded the Winchester's magazine and brought it to bear on the hillside above him.

"Come on, Wade!" Billy called to his friend.

As Billy fired at his hidden enemies, Wade and young Jason McNally rushed toward the gully. Shells splintered cedar limbs and ricocheted wildly off rocks. Wade flew into the gully, followed seconds later by Jason.

"Wade, how's your ammunition?" Billy asked his friend.

"I got enough to keep 'em busy awhile," Wade answered. "But it might get a little lonely on toward nightfall."

"McNally, how many horses did you see?" Billy asked as the firing resumed.

"Must be a hundred at least," Jason said excitedly.

"No chance of that," Billy said. "How many did you actually *see*?"

"Ten, maybe fifteen," the young man said, huddling beside Wade Bennett.

"They'll rush our position," Billy said. "Wade, you cover us from the south. McNally, watch the northeast. I'll take the northwest."

Wade nodded, and Jason pointed his rifle through the rocks. A flurry of gunfire followed, and Wade cried out in pain.

"You all right?" Billy asked.

"Just great," Wade said, holding his left forearm. Blood flowed between his fingers.

"Bad?" Billy asked.

"I'll live awhile yet," Wade said as the men on the hillside sent another volley into the gully.

"I'll bind it for you," Billy said, setting down his rifle for a moment.

"McNally, open up on anything that moves."

"I can't," Jason said, cowering behind the rocks.

"I'm not asking you to milk a cow or ride to town, man!" Billy shouted, shaking the boy by the collar. "We're going to die here if you don't snap out of it!"

"We'll all die anyway," Jason whimpered.

"Then there'll be a price to be paid," Billy said, his eyes flashing with a rage that frightened young McNally even more than the band of bushwhackers.

As Billy bound Wade's arm, Jason fired at the shadowy figures on the hillside.

"You boys might as well give it up!" a voice called out from the hill. "We'll finish you come nightfall."

"Come do it now!" Billy yelled. "A lot of men're going to die here if you try anything after dark."

"We can't hold out here," Jason said. "We'd better give up."

"Ever hear of anyone taking prisoners in a range war, Wade?" Billy asked.

"Not that I know about," Wade said.

"If you haven't got the guts to come down after us, go home, farmer!" Billy cried out. "If you've got a need to get yourselves shot, come on!"

The hillside erupted with firing and the ground around the gully was spattered with bullets. Several men raced down the hill and Billy coldly fixed them in his sights. First one, then a second man fell backward. A third was picked off by Wade Bennett, and another was hit by Jason McNally.

"That'll even the odds some," Wade said, smiling.

"Too early to get excited," Billy told his friend. "I'm down to seven shells, plus what's in my Colt. You?"

"I've got a couple of dozen left," Wade said, handing over some to Billy.

"I'm about out, but there's a full box in my saddlebags," Jason said.

Billy and Wade exchanged looks.

"We can't hold 'em off without

shells," Billy said grimly. "I'm on my way."

"You can keep your gun firing faster than I can," Wade said. "I'll go."

Billy reluctantly swung his rifle around and gave Wade covering fire. But the mechanism jammed, leaving Wade in the open, shielded only by Jason McNally's occasional shot.

"Give me that!" Billy screamed, tearing the rifle away from young McNally. It was too late, though. As Wade grabbed the box from Jason's saddlebag, two shots fired in rapid succession found their mark.

"Billy?" Wade cried out, stumbling a few steps before falling.

Billy dropped the rifle and charged out into the open. He fired his pistol as he went. Two men stepped out from shelter to fire, but Billy hit them both. He reached Wade, slung his friend over one shoulder, and prepared to start back for the gully. Jason fired Wade's rifle at the hillside, scattering the remaining ambushers. Billy managed to pick up the box of shells and head for safety.

When they returned to the gully, Billy set Wade down and began tending his friend's wounds.

"The gun jammed," Billy explained, wiping the sweat from Wade's face. "I'm sorry."

"Wasn't your fault," Wade mumbled. "You did what you could."

"I'm always doing what I can, but it's never enough," Billy said, staring toward the hidden gunmen as the shooting resumed.

"Like at Shiloh?" Wade asked, coughing as he spoke. "Was it like that for my father?"

"And mine." Billy sighed.

"So now it's our turn, Willie Delamer," Wade said, trying to smile. "Don't mind me calling you that, do you?"

"Doesn't make a lot of difference now, I suppose."

"Things'll be better when we get to Colorado, won't they? Tell me about that place we're going to buy. Tell me about the house. Tell me . . . "

The sentence was never completed. Billy felt a strangeness in the air. Wade's eyes fixed on the sky, and Billy shuddered.

"Wade!" Billy screamed.

There was no answer, though. Billy cradled his friend's head for a minute, then rested it on the cold, hard ground.

"Is he . . . " Jason asked.

"Yes," Billy said, blinking away what might have become a tear. Then he methodically reloaded Jason's Winchester.

"What do we do now?" Jason asked.

"Kill them," Billy said, staring with fury at the flashes coming from the hillside. It was nearly dusk. It was already difficult to see. A single man weaving from rock to rock would be almost invisible.

"What are you doing?" Jason asked as Billy began crawling toward the far end of the gully.

"What you said you were paying me for," Billy told the boy. "I'm going to empty that hillside."

"They'll shoot you," Jason warned. "That's crazy!"

But Billy was beyond fear, beyond caution. He continued on, creeping through the rocks as the assassins on the hillside continued firing at the gully. All earlier doubts were gone. He was in his element, crossing the rocky ridge as he had at Shiloh, at Little Round Top, in the wilderness. He was like a ghost, darting through the shadows until he gained the crest of the hillside. Below, four figures could be detected, rising to fire, then slipping back behind cover.

Billy opened up on them, firing as rapidly as he could move the lever of the rifle. The first of the ambushers cried out, then tumbled crazily down the hillside. Another clutched his side and collapsed. Two others scrambled off through the brush.

"They're behind us!" one of the men cried out. "Run for your lives!"

There was no one else around to heed the warning. The two remaining ambushers managed to mount horses and escape. Billy called down to Jason that it was clear, then walked to where two of the would-be assassins lay wounded.

"Don't shoot," they pleaded.

"I don't have to," Billy said, collecting their weapons. "The wolves'll finish you off tonight."

"No, please," one of them begged. "I've got a wife and two kids at home."

"You thought of that too late," Billy said, spitting on the ground. "Nothing can help you now."

Billy rounded up the rest of the weapons and rolled them in a blanket. He then tied the guns onto the back of a horse, gently tied Wade Bennett onto a second, and saddled Bluebonnet.

"Starr?" Jason asked.

"Leave us alone just a minute," Billy said, motioning toward Wade's limp body.

"You all right?" Jason asked, pointing to a bright red stain that was spreading across Billy's shoulder.

"Fine," Billy said, only now feeling the sting of the lead ball lodged against his shoulder blade. He ignored the bleeding and looked into Wade's still eyes. "You just rest easy, Wade," Billy whispered. "It won't be long now till you can rest."

"Starr," Jason said, shaking Billy's uninjured arm. "He's dead."

"Don't you think I know that?" Billy asked, his eyes filling with rage. "Don't you know we were friends?"

"You're bleeding," Jason said.

"I've bled before. Help me get the others onto their horses."

The two of them gathered up their three lifeless companions and tied them on their horses' backs. Billy gathered the reins of the animals, then led them to where Jason stood waiting.

"Better bind that shoulder," Jason said, handing Billy a strip of white cloth.

"Thanks," Billy said, folding the cloth into a neat square, then pressing it against the tender flesh. He next tore his shirt into strips in order to hold the dressing in place. The bleeding stopped, and though a throbbing pain spread through his shoulder, he nevertheless got into the saddle.

"Doesn't it hurt?" Jason asked.

"Of course," Billy said, gritting his teeth as the pain sent tremors through his arm. "But pain's a small thing once you get accustomed to it."

"Get used to it?"

"There's not much to it when you stack it against the killing. A man feels pain getting his fingers too close to a fire. Pain? No, it's not so much."

"And the killing?"

"It lingers like something growing and festering. And it never goes far away."

Billy's eyes died a little as he spoke, and Jason shivered. It was clear the young man didn't feel at ease in the company of Billy Starr.

"Come on," Billy said, starting out. They rode on, leading the other horses.

They rode two miles or so toward

the ranch when they met a pair of drovers.

"What happened?" asked the first, a Texan named King.

"Ambushed," Billy told them, handing over the other horses' reins. "Best send someone back to bring in the mustangs." Turning to Jason, Billy said, "Tell your pa I'll be on along."

"Where are you going?" Jason asked.

"After the others," Billy said, reloading the Winchester.

"So what do I do with them?" Jason asked, pointing to the four dead riders.

"Take them back to the ranch. Unless you plan to come along."

"You don't know my pa too well. If I go back and tell him you went after the others alone, he'll turn me over to John."

"John?" Billy said, spitting.

"He doesn't like you much, either."

"He's going to wind up dead one of these days. He wants it so bad he can taste it. He'll be dead long before you are, unless you aren't careful tonight."

"John's been mean since the day he was born." Jason sighed. "But he's fast with a gun."

"There's a lot of difference between shooting rocks off a corral fence and killing a man. Let's go."

"Go where? Do you know where they are?" Jason asked.

"I started tracking animals when I was five," Billy said, laughing in a somber sort of way. "Come on." He nodded to the drovers and swung his horse around.

They rode a mile or two, following a trail that was easy to read in the moonlight.

"They flew out of here like the devil himself was after them," Jason said. "Even I could follow them."

"You want to know something about the devil?" Billy asked.

"What's that?" Jason asked.

"He is after them," Billy said, his eyes blazing in the moonlight.

Jason shivered a bit then, and Billy laughed. Then the trail vanished, and he motioned for his companion to be silent.

"Not far now," Billy whispered.

They continued for another quarter mile. Then Billy signalled to Jason to halt. They climbed off their horses, and Billy tied Bluebonnet's reins to an oak sapling.

"What are you doing?" Jason asked. "They could be another five miles from here."

"No, just over the next rise," Billy said.

"You don't know that."

"I don't?" Billy said, shaking his head. "Look, boy, I can smell them from here. If you'd use your senses, even you might pick up the odor of smoke in the air."

"But – "

"If you're coming with me, follow closely. If not, get out of here."

"Why not just ride down on them?"

"Sometimes you meet up with an unpleasant surprise that way," Billy said, creeping forward.

Jason followed Billy across a low ridge. Below them a single campfire burned. Blankets were spread out on each side of the fire. A rifle protruded from behind a nearby cottonwood.

"You see?" Billy said, pointing at what appeared to be the guard. "You'd ride down there and shoot that man wouldn't you? And then the ones in the shadows would kill you."

"In the shadows?" Jason asked. "I can see them sleeping."

"I've used that same trick, McNally. Men breathe. You see those blankets moving? Now listen carefully. I want you to watch the rifle. When I get to that big rock across camp, you shoot. Got it, McNally?"

"And then?"

"I'll get the others," Billy said.

"All of them?"

"All. It's called a blood debt."

"For Wade? I owe 'em for my ma, too," Jason said.

"You're welcome to any that get by me."

Billy didn't wait for an answer. He just started across the hillside toward the enemy camp. It was not easy going, but he moved like a snake, doing little more than stirring the brush. When he reached the rock, a shot rang out. The rifle behind the cottonwood dropped to the ground, and a false figure made of a saddle, blanket, and hat disintegrated.

The others waited for a moment, then returned Jason's fire. Billy counted two rifles. After marking each one's position, he opened fire. Each of the men in turn tumbled from his hiding place, dead or dying. Billy didn't bother to determine which.

"Let's get back to the ranch," Billy called to Jason. "They'll have friends out looking for them by morning. And your father will be anxious."

"He won't worry about me." Jason sighed. "I'm the younger brother, you see."

"Oh?" Billy said. "That makes a difference to him, does it?"

"All the difference. Second sons are nothing."

Billy glanced off at the sky, remembering how it'd been for him.

"Tell me something," Jason said. "You suppose you could teach me to handle a pistol like you do? I'd pay to learn."

"Why would you want to learn?"

"To prove to Pa I'm as good as John."

"Oh. And would you shoot your brother down for the dog he is?"

"He's not a dog!" Jason shouted. "He's got a mean streak is all."

"You couldn't," Billy said, smiling. "Look, I'll tell you something. You know what it takes to be fast, to be the best?"

"Like you?"

"Sure, like Billy Starr. It takes a heart so cold it smells of death. It takes eyes like mine, eyes that don't see anyone, just shams. If something happened to you tonight, there'd be those who'd mourn you. Me, they'd just roll what was left of me into a hole and forget me.

"I won't teach you to shoot, McNally. I wouldn't want anyone to turn down my road who's got something left inside him. A man starts out alone on my path, and he stays that way. Oh, friends may come along. He might even love a woman. But sooner or later they drift away or get shot."

"Mike Dunstan's your friend."

"Dunstan?" Billy said, laughing. "He's never had a friend. He spends people like gold pieces. They're only good for what they get him. No, I'm on my own."

As they headed on down the road, Billy thought to himself that it was better that way, better not to reach out, like with Ellen, like with Wade Bennett. Once again he was terribly alone. And once again the past was buried in the silent guarantee that death brought.

12

BILLY didn't remember riding the last mile or so back to the ranch. When he awoke, he found himself resting in the bunkhouse. Someone had washed him, and his shoulder had been bound tightly. Young Miguel stood beside the bed, and an eerie silence hung in the air.

"Where are the others?" Billy mumbled.

"Gone, señor," Miguel told him. "They go with Señor Jason to find those who shot you."

"That's been attended to," Billy said, the memory of the night before flashing through his mind.

"Señor McNally, he say there are still many near the town who will pay for the shooting of our men."

"Then it's war all over again." Billy sighed. He tried to sit up, but pain exploded through his shoulder at the slightest movement.

"You should not move so much, señor," Miguel warned. "You have much fever."

"The bullet's still in there, isn't it?" Billy asked. "What kind of man leaves me lying here with a bullet inside me while he chases a bunch of farmers off the range? Get my horse."

"You can't ride, señor," Miguel said, holding Billy still. "Your head is full of clouds. You wait for Señor Dunstan to return."

"No," Billy said, struggling to get up.

But Miguel was right. Billy was out of his head, and he lacked the determination to make up for the loss of blood and the fever raging through his body. He collapsed onto the bed, then drifted.

Billy's mind swept him across battlefields, returned him to summer days spent fishing along the Brazos. It was a simpler, kinder time. It disappeared amid the terrible nightmare that had been his reality for the past nine years. He shrank back in horror as the Michigan cavalry swept the field at Five Forks. He saw himself fighting with a bayonet at Shiloh after the regiment had exhausted its ammunition.

Faces paraded through his memory. Men killed, men shot, men devoured by the monster that seemed forever at his side, casting a shadow of death across everything Billy touched, all that he loved, everyone who had loved him.

"It would have been better to die in Corinth," Billy mumbled. Die before the smell of death grew to swallow all that remained of him.

"Señor?" Miquel asked.

"It's all right," Billy said. "My head wanders."

"Señor, someone comes," Miguel said, trembling slightly.

"Get my gun," Billy said, fighting the pain and dizziness in order to get to his feet.

Leaning on Miguel, Billy managed to limp to the door of the bunkhouse.

There, rolling to a stop before the house, was a wagon. Billy's legs wobbled as he searched for its occupants.

"We came to take you to town," Dunstan called out.

"It is all right, señor," Miguel whispered. "It is Señor Dunstan."

Two men walked over and took Billy in their arms. He felt himself go limp, and the pistol dropped from his fingers. His eyes tried to focus, but it was hopeless.

"I take care of this for you, señor," Miguel said, rubbing the long barrel of the revolver against his shirt. "I clean it for you good, Señor Starr."

Billy heard him only faintly. His mind was back in Texas: seeing, feeling, remembering.

"Ellen?" he called out.

"He's pure out of his skull," one of Dunstan's men said. "Best get him to town fast."

The men carried Billy to the wagon and laid him gently on a pair of blankets. The driver whipped the horses into action, and the wagon bounced along the dusty road toward town. Blood seeped through the bandages on Billy's shoulder. Small red drops stained the bed of the wagon, leaked through the boards, and spotted the sandy ground below. But Billy's pale face showed no emotion. The fever had carried him away.

When his vision finally cleared, Billy saw a shadowy face leaning over him. The fire was gone from his shoulder, and there was a softness all around him. Feathers. A bed with a mattress. Even a pillow. And there was a foreign scent in the air, a wonderfully feminine smell. Perfume. Not like in the bawdy houses of Abilene, either. This was a richer, more genuine flavor he remembered from the manor houses of Mississippi and Virginia.

"Hello," said a soft voice. "It's about time you came around."

"What?" Billy asked, his forehead wrinkling as he fought to bring his eyes into focus.

"You're perfectly safe," the voice told him. "Your friends brought you to town."

"The bullet," Billy said, breathing heavily.

"I took it out. Don't worry. I didn't cut the muscles, not so much as a tendon. I'm quite skilful with a knife. My grandfather was a surgeon."

"But . . . who . . ."

"I'll answer all your questions, Mr. Starr, but later. Now you need your rest. I'm going to leave you to my brother. I've got a business to run."

"Ellen?" Billy cried out, grabbing the soft hands as the figure started to leave.

"There, there," the voice said. "I'm not Ellen. I do have to go, but when you're a little stronger, I'll explain it all. Now lie back. If you need anything, my brother will be here."

He heard her departing footsteps. Another, lighter series of steps followed. They stopped, and a slight-framed figure sat down.

"She'll be back after a while to look in on you," said a new voice that cracked with the onset of manhood. "She never stays gone too long."

Billy heard nothing more. His mind drifted back to a cloudlike unreality. When his head cleared again, he felt a soft hand on his forehead. He opened his eyes, and the fog began to lift.

"You're better," the tender voice said. "The fever's broken."

Billy turned to one side, then groaned as pain throbbed through his chest.

"You shouldn't move just yet, Mr. Starr," the voice told him. "You've got several days of resting ahead of you. You're lucky to be alive. Another few hours with that lead inside you and Reverend Simpson would have been reading over your headstone for certain."

"They should've taken it out when I got back," Billy said, frowning.

"Lucky they didn't. Dunstan's killed two or three men cutting on them. And left another maimed. Mrs. McNally could have done it for you. Her hands were steady as a rock. You've done a lot of bleeding. Those cowhands would've killed you for sure."

"You have a light touch," Billy said, intertwining his fingers with hers.

"You'd best keep your mind on the business at hand," she said, slipping away. "Has your stomach settled enough to take in some soup?"

"It's the only way to get stronger," Billy said.

"I'll ask Douglas to help you sit up. Be back directly."

"Wait," Billy pleaded, fighting to clear his vision. "I don't even know your name."

"Oh, but we've met, Mr. Starr. I'm Jessica Hart."

An image appeared in Billy's mind. Yes, the girl who ran the mercantile. But he couldn't recall her eyes, the color of her hair. And there was an urgency inside him to know and see everything about her.

Billy stared at the ceiling through

watering eyes. He blinked away the film that covered them. With his good right hand, he rubbed them until the focus returned. And as footsteps disturbed the silence, he glanced at the door.

It wasn't her, though. Instead he saw a slim-shouldered boy of fourteen or so, dark-haired, with the shadow of a mustache on his upper lip.

"You've come back to the living, huh?" the boy asked. "Jessie said to help you sit up. It's going to hurt a lot. Sure you want to try it?"

"Come on, boy," Billy said.

"Name's Doug," the young man said.

"Well, Doug, give me a hand," Billy urged, rising forward.

Douglas slipped the pillow back against the headboard of the bed, then eased Billy into a sitting position. Billy's breathing grew labored, and a dizziness returned to his head.

"You must be awful strong, mister," Doug said, wiping the sweat from Billy's forehead. "I've seen lots of men shot up. Grandpa did a lot of cutting during the war. Most in your shape would have died."

"What war was that?"

"The rebellion. We lived in Virginia, in the Shenandoah Valley. Grandpa treated soldiers on both sides. Ma, too. She died from a fever there. I used to bring the men water. And help drag away the dead ones."

"Your sister, too?"

"They called her the angel of mercy. It marked her, though. She's got a natural soft spot for men in pain."

"And you?"

"I look out for her," the boy explained. "Softness gets whittled away out here. That's what happened to Pa. He was a teacher in Lexington. The war took that away, so we came out here and opened a store."

"And he died?" Billy asked.

"Like most do." Doug sighed. "Be careful with her, mister. She's important. I've seen men come to this town and take a woman for granted. She's not one of those ladies that live on the ground floor of the hotel."

"I know that."

"You know about pain. I can see that easy enough. Don't bring her any grief. I'd shoot you before I'd have that."

"I won't bring her any harm, boy," Billy promised. "I rode through the valley myself. I've seen more than my share of broken people."

"Long as we understand each other," Doug said. "And I haven't been a boy since Pa died. My name's Doug or Mr. Hart."

"Believe I'm going to like you, Doug," Billy said, smiling.

"Liable to be a one-sided kind of liking," Doug answered with a scowl.

The floorboards creaked then, and Jessica entered the room, carrying a bowl of soup balanced carefully on a wooden tray.

"Mind the store, Douglas," she told her brother.

"I can feed the man," Doug said.

"Douglas," she said firmly.

"Yes, Jessie," the boy conceded, retiring.

"I don't need anyone to feed me," Billy said, taking the spoon from her.

"No, but I thought you might like some company," she said. "Douglas can be a bit crusty. He hovers over me like a mother hen sometimes."

"Be glad he's around," Billy said, staring at her face. "There's those who'd take advantage of a woman as pretty as you."

"Mr. Starr, I'll warn you. There's a shotgun just outside the door. And I might not be as gentle removing lead I put into a man."

"I wouldn't push myself on a person," Billy said, his eyes turning away from her.

"I can tell that," she said.

As Billy sipped the soup, he stared at the face in front of him. There was a simple beauty to it, a kind of grace born of gentleness. Her deep blue eyes revealed a sensitivity he thought he'd lost forever when he left Ellen behind in Texas. And her thin lips were delicate, so soft . . .

Her body was not as frail as he'd thought at first. It was lithe, taut as a rope in some ways, yet nimble like a willow. Her soft blond hair was worn long so that it fell against his arm when she removed the empty bowl.

"Would you like some more?" she asked.

"No, thank you, ma' am."

"It's Jessica," she said, smiling. "Jessie to my friends."

"Jessie," he said, pronouncing the name with a sweetness, a softness he'd thought lost forever.

"Is there anything else I can do for you?" she asked. "Are you warm enough?"

"With you here," he said. "Could you sit with me awhile?"

"Later," she told him. "I have to attend to the store accounts. I'll send Douglas up."

"I'm fine."

"No, you've been in the dark for two

days. You need company. Besides, he's not a bad checker player, and he's in need of a man's conversation. He gets too much of me."

"I envy him," Billy said, admiring her smile.

"Best curb your tongue, sir," she said, easing her way out of the room.

Doug came in a short while later, not with a checkerboard but with a pack of playing cards.

"I remember you played with Luke Hall," Doug said. "They say you're good."

"Good enough," Billy admitted.

"You killed him quick that day," Doug said quietly, almost reverently. "Are you always so cold about it?"

"Always," Billy said, shuddering as he felt the darkness descending on him again.

"Sorry," Doug said, sitting beside the bed. "I shouldn't have brought it back to you."

"It's never far," Billy said. "Deal the cards."

13

BILLY fought his way awake that night. He found himself sweating, screaming out into the darkness. A soft hand touched his right arm, and he clung to it.

"Ellen, help me!" he cried out, tears flowing down his cheeks. "Ellen!"

"She's not here," the gentle voice of Jessie Hart told him. "Calm down now. You're having a nightmare."

"What?" Billy asked, blinking away the tears. "Oh, it's you," he said, finally recognizing her face in the dimly lit room.

"Everything's all right," she said soothingly. "Everything. Now rest easy, and I'll sponge your forehead."

Billy relaxed the tight muscles in his arms, and she tenderly bathed his face and chest. He felt like a small child tended by a mother's loving hands. He was used to doing for himself. But there was something terribly reassuring about Jessie's touch and a special sparkle in her eyes that erased his troubles.

"Tell me about her, Mr. Starr," she said.

"Call me Billy," he said, trying to mirror her smile.

"Billy," she whispered, widening her grin so that her dazzling ivory teeth gleamed in the moonlight. "What was she like, this Ellen of yours?"

"Soft, like you," he explained. "And hard, too. She had a special inner strength. She always understood what I was thinking, how I felt."

"What happened to her?"

He frowned as the memory of that last time together filled his mind. He watched her waving good-bye as he set out on the cattle drive that would carry him away from his beloved Brazos forever.

"She died," Billy muttered, closing his eyes for a minute so she wouldn't read the lie that was written there.

"You can tell me the truth, Billy. I've been listening to you for three nights now. You keep saying you're sorry. You talk of farewells."

"Haven't you ever said good-bye to someone who died?" he asked.

"Not and talk about how sorry I was that I went away. You left her behind, didn't you?"

"Not exactly. I meant to come back. I intended it that way. But something happened to me."

Billy let the words hang in the air for several minutes. Then he sadly stared out the window.

"*I* died," he mumbled.

She gently turned his head toward her and gazed with wide eyes at his face.

"You what?" she gasped.

"I died," he repeated. "I became somebody else."

"I don't understand."

"It's not a thing that can be shared," Billy said, trembling. "Dying's a personal thing."

"You're still very much alive, Billy Starr."

"Sure, Billy Starr, gunman, killer."

"Who are you?" she asked, sitting beside him on the edge of the bed.

Billy's eyes changed. They were cold, lifeless. It was a sad transformation, a sort of second death.

"You're terribly old, aren't you?" Jessie asked. "You look almost like a boy, like Douglas, in your sleep. But when you wake, all the gentleness vanishes."

"It wasn't my doing," Billy told her. "It comes of being shot at, stabbed, chased after, and hunted down. It's because a man needs to belong to someone, someplace. And once he's cut away from that, he's just a seed blowing in the summer breeze. Except even a seed plants itself somewhere, grows, becomes something. A man, well, he just wanders."

There was sadness in Jessie's eyes, too, as she held his hand. She felt something more than sympathy. Perhaps it was a touch of understanding. Whatever, she didn't let go of him.

"I've mended a lot of broken men in my life," she told Billy. "In Virginia, I watched an entire army die. I saw the boy I would have married charge across a field because Yankees were burning our house. I watched him being shot down by men who laughed."

"I've laughed as I've shot," Billy said. "I laughed because I couldn't cry. I laughed because the hardness in me wouldn't allow anything else."

"Those men laughed because they enjoyed it," Jessie said. "And Johnny was fourteen, a month younger than Douglas is now."

Billy read the sadness on her face, the terrible pain that flowed out of her. He touched her hair with his fingers and allowed her to ease onto the bed beside him.

"I've killed a lot of men," Billy whispered. "I've seen more death than life. I'm hollow, not much of a man at all. I've never enjoyed it, though.

I always smell the sickness, the awful waste that comes of killing."

"You could put it behind you. Take a new name, go somewhere else."

"I've tried." Billy sighed, a great lump growing in his throat. "God, how I've tried. I've gone to the mountains and roamed the plains. I've sought out the Indians, gone off by myself, but the killing always finds me."

"It doesn't have to," she said. "I'll help you find a way out. I'll help you forget, Billy. Starting over's not that bad."

"It's not the starting that's hard," he told her. "It's staying with it."

"Then we'll stay with it," she said, leaning over and kissing his forehead. "There's good in you, Billy Starr. I've touched it. Together we'll manage."

Together. The word rolled through Billy's head, growing louder and louder. It multiplied until it exploded through his insides. In the midst of that explosion was one instant when he glimpsed a second chance, a fresh start.

It was that picture of a different Billy that he read in her eyes.

"I'll try," he promised.

"And I'll help," she said. "Leave it to me. We'll make you over."

But when Jessie left, the fear returned. He knew too well what had always happened before, even in the camps of the Cheyenne, in the high mountains. In Abilene and Dodge City. He wondered if it would ever be possible to turn away from such a past.

The next morning Jessie and her brother helped Billy walk down the stairs to a small room behind the store. A stove occupied one corner, and a round table filled the center of the room.

Billy was surprised at the weakness that possessed his legs, at the lack of power in his movements. He'd never felt so decrepit, not even after Shiloh.

"It's the loss of blood," Jessie explained as she started their breakfast. "You can't expect to wrestle a bear your first day up. By the end of the week the stiffness should be gone. You can start exercising then."

"I've never in my whole life been laid up more 'n a day or two by anything," Billy objected. "I'll be walking on my own this afternoon. Tomorrow I'll begin working the shoulder."

"It needs rest," Jessie told him. "I know about such things."

"Then you know how a shoulder can tighten up on a man if he doesn't use it. A one-armed man's no good. I've brought it around before. Takes time, but for every day you wait, it just gets that much worse."

"It will hurt," she warned. "Hurt bad."

"I've hurt before," he said "Now, what's for breakfast?"

Billy had expected her to be upset, but he could tell deep down that she would have been disappointed by any other reaction. He noticed a smile of approval on young Doug's face, too. After a breakfast of salted bacon and fresh eggs, Billy sat at the table and started stretching the sore tendons of his shoulder.

"You've seen it done before," Jessie said, watching Billy press and probe the inflamed flesh with the fingers of his right hand.

"You did the cutting," Billy said. "You must've noticed this isn't the only hole in my hide."

"I don't miss much. There were saber scars on your legs. From the war?"

"Cavalry, ma'am," Billy said, giving her a mock bow.

"You were young."

"Sixteen at Shiloh."

"Did you fight at Gettysburg, Billy?" Doug asked. "That's where Grandpa was killed. My brother Nathan, too."

"I was there," Billy told them. "With Hood on the right flank."

"You're from Texas, then," Jessie said. "We passed through part of the state on the way here."

"Why'd you stop in such country as this?" Billy asked. "This is a heartless kind of land. On over in Colorado, now, there are mountains that make the Blue Ridge seem like anthills. It's a beautiful country. Just beginning to grow."

"This country will grow, too, Billy. But only when the churches and the schools take over; when the guns are put away."

"I've been places where they've had all the schools and churches you could imagine," Billy said with a scowl. "Judges and sheriffs who stole a man's land with one hand and locked him in jail with the other. Laws! Laws can rob a man of what's his, even of himself."

"There are laws and laws. You're not the only one who ever lost something to carpetbaggers. That's right, too, isn't it? I saw the look on your face when Dunstan shot that Judge Fulton."

"We heard all about Fulton," Doug explained. "He was chased down the Brazos by some cattlemen. He was trying to build his own kingdom here on the Cimarron."

"So now he's found himself another

kind of kingdom," Billy said, laughing grimly.

"Where will you find yourself, Billy?" Jessie asked.

"Likely there beside him," Billy said, quivering. "He'll probably be collecting a dying tax for the devil."

That afternoon found Billy still in the back room, limbering his shoulder, making it ready for work again. His head had begun to clear, and as he ate, the strength returned to his legs.

"Never heard anyone so bitter in all my life as you, Billy," Jessie remarked as she rolled out dough for the day's baking. "You hate just about everybody, don't you?"

"I don't know that I hate anyone," Billy said, scratching his head. "Well, maybe one man."

"Your brother?" she asked.

"You sure know a lot of things," he said after a moment, gazing at her with suspicion.

"You talk too much in your sleep," she told him.

"Well, I suppose you know just about all of it, then."

"Why don't you talk it over with me?"

"I did that with Wade Bennett," Billy said, staring at his feet. "I ended up killing men because of it. I don't want anyone ever again to know the whole of it."

"All right," she said, pounding the dough with her rolling pin. "But tell me why you left Ellen. You loved her."

"From the first time we chased each other through the Brazos." Billy sighed.

"Then why?"

"It's complicated, Jessie."

"Tell me."

"I came back from the war expecting everything to be like it was before. It wasn't. My brother Sam had taken over. The places, the people I'd grown up with were all changed. My parents were dead. Most of our old friends were being chased off their land by Sam."

"How?"

"He used that judge, Jessie. If Sam didn't fence them off their land, he'd get that Yank judge to raise the taxes past what could be paid."

"And you fought him."

"For a time. I thought maybe we'd come to terms, that we could combine our talents. I saved his life, Jessie! And he hired a man to kill me."

"What?"

"See, it came down to a choice. If I stayed, I'd have to kill my own brother. Or be killed by him."

"And?"

"I couldn't do it, Jessie. Not that I'm not hard enough to shoot a man. But killing Sam? How could I do that and still hold my head up? My family stands for something. Or did. How could I have faced Sam's children? What sort of life could Ellen and I have built knowing it rested on the corpse of my own brother?"

"You could have taken her away," Jessie said.

"She'd never've been happy. A woman like Ellen needs her roots. I ran hard for more'n a year."

"You sacrificed a lot, Billy. For what?"

"Maybe for nothing," he said sadly. "I hope it was for my youngest brother, so Ellen could have a real life and so the family would go on."

"You're a fool, Billy," Jessie told him. "Running from a thing you want so much! And to what? A pistol?"

"Do you understand now why I said I died?"

Her face grew pale, and she nodded.

"I fought for four years, crossed half the continent in a fifth, all just to come back to something that had changed," Billy said, choking on the words. "Maybe I wanted to find a part of myself. But that was gone, too. The war did it, I suppose, as much as Sam or anyone else. I watched whole ridges of men shot down. Rivers of blood flowed where corn used to grow."

"I know all about it," she said, rubbing her eyes. "We lived in New Market."

"It did something to me, Jessie, turned me inside out. Maybe if Mama had been there when I came back; maybe if I'd let Sam die instead of saving him from a stampede; maybe if I'd done lots of things different, I could have stayed. But I didn't, and now I'm what I am."

"So now what?"

"I go back to McNally's ranch."

"Billy, do you know what's going on? Do you know what Dunstan and his men are doing? Ever since the killing out in the canyon, farms have been burned nightly. Sometimes there's a lot of shooting. Other times a family just up and disappears. Little children, Billy! Women!"

"So the farmers say. You forget Mrs. McNally was shot by somebody, too."

"Tell me, Billy. Have you ever shot a woman? A little girl?"

"No!" he said angrily. "But I close

to shot a boy holding a shotgun one night. You see, Jessie, he would've killed me, shot me down without a second thought."

"Little Frank Gunnison staggered in here last night," she said, pounding the dough again. "He's ten years old! He stumbled inside the store, white as a sheet. When I finally got him to talk, he told how they rode his folks down without so much as a whisper of explanation. His little sister, too. She was six and extremely dangerous."

"I wasn't there. Neither were you. You don't know for certain how it happened."

"Oh, Billy," she said, slamming her hand against the table. "If you go back to Dunstan, you'll go back to the killing, too. It could be different."

"How?" Billy asked.

"Stay here with me. Put your guns away."

"A man has to make his living."

"There's plenty of work here."

"I'm no storekeeper, Jessie. Besides,

if I ever put the guns away, it has to be out there. I've done all the running I plan to."

"Go somewhere with me before you leave. Please?" she asked finally.

"Sure," he agreed.

He didn't learn what she had in mind for a couple of days. Then, bright and early Sunday morning, she led him down the street to the simple wooden church. As he sat beside her on a hard oak bench, he couldn't have felt more uncomfortable. He hadn't been in a regular church since they'd buried his colonel in Richmond six years before.

The farmers and townspeople who filled the church didn't help matters. Their hostile glances sent icy chills down Billy's spine.'

"They don't want me here," Billy whispered to Jessie.

"All people are welcome in God's house," she told him.

I wonder, Billy thought, as he

observed the cold gray eyes of the woman across the aisle. He asked himself if her husband had been one of the men who'd shot bullets at him only a few days ago. The front two benches were filled with ragged children. Billy avoided their eyes, hoping his Winchester hadn't made them orphans.

The worship service itself was conducted by a Methodist circuit preacher named Simpson. The reverend was short, a little on the fat side, but his face held a kind of sincerity that drew a man's confidence.

"I'm pleased to find you among us, Mr. Starr," the reverend said as he passed Billy. "We all thank the Lord that you have safely passed through your hour of torment and affliction."

"Thank you, sir," Billy said.

"Perhaps you will repent your vile and evil ways," a woman behind him said.

"At least he didn't wear his gun in here," another added.

"I never promised it would be easy," Jessie said, squeezing his hand as Billy tensed.

Normally he would have replied, shouted back to the farmers that he'd never fired the first shot in a quarrel, that before he'd killed anyone, three McNally hands had lain dead. But he kept his silence. And as the service continued, he felt himself being transported back to a simpler time of his life, an age when he'd believed in things and people. When two small boys rang the bells announcing the conclusion of the meeting, there was something new and bright in Billy's eyes.

"It did help," Jessie said as they walked out together onto Front Street.

"Yes." he sighed.

Billy didn't ride to the McNally ranch that afternoon as he'd planned. Instead he returned to the little room in back of the store. A strange peacefulness settled in around him that night. After blowing out the candle that lit the room, he stared out into the night sky, feeling closer to the stars than at any time he could immediately recall.

Just as Billy's eyelids began to close, the door opened, and young Douglas Hart slipped into the room.

"Trouble?" Billy asked, sitting up.

"What makes you think that?" Doug asked, sitting on the floor beside Billy's bed.

"It's been a while since you felt you needed to keep a watch over me at night," Billy pointed out.

"I came to say something," Doug explained. "It's about Jessie. I think she loves you. She for sure cares a lot about what happens to you."

"I care about her, too," Billy admitted.

"I wouldn't want her getting hurt."

"I think we had this talk," Billy said, smiling at the young man who suddenly appeared taller. "I wouldn't hurt her. Not for the world."

"If you really mean that, you'll ride away from here tomorrow. If you stay, she'll get too serious."

"She's not a child, Doug. Don't you suppose she's old enough to make up her own mind about something like that?"

"She has," Doug said, frowning. "She thinks you can quit."

"And you don't?"

"Wish you could," he said, looking away from Billy. "But I've seen you shoot. Sooner or later you'll go back to it. I like you, Billy. You make Jessie laugh. But it's not worth the crying she'll be doing later on."

"I'll do it," Billy promised. "I'll leave in the morning. I'll try to stay away. If I can't, then we'll have to talk more on it."

"And the killing?"

"I'm going to do my best to escape it. I don't know that I can. It's like a shadow chasing me. It always catches up. But who'd've thought I'd be sitting in that church this morning?"

Doug's eyes brightened, and a hint of friendliness appeared on his youthful face.

"I won't make a promise I can't keep, Doug," Billy told the boy. "I'll do my best."

"I know you will," Doug said. "But I don't think it'll be enough."

14

BILLY rode back to the ranch slowly. The stiffness in his shoulder had not yet gone away, and he grew a bit lightheaded. His thoughts wandered. Still, he'd spent ten days in Cimarron City, and it was time to return to business.

His stay with Jessie Hart had provided a rare interlude of peace, a precious chance to forget what he had become and enjoy a taste of what might have been. He found himself missing Ellen less and longing for Jessie more.

But Billy knew what he'd said to her had been right. If there was ever to be an escape for him from the guns, from the violence, it had to come from stepping away. Running would never do. A man might hide from his enemies, but never from himself.

Billy found the ranch changed. The

house and other buildings had received a fresh coat of paint. A new corral had been built, and there was more than a little activity. Men buzzed about like bees in a hive.

"Howdy, Starr," Jack Manning said to Billy as he rode up. "How's the arm?"

"Still stiff," Billy said, rubbing his shoulder. "But a man can only stay on the shelf so long before he turns rusty."

"Guess so," Jack agreed, laughing.

"You've been busy," Billy told him.

"Cattle drives coming. Got to get ready for seven thousand head at least. More next year. We cleared out some obstacles, too."

"Obstacles?" Billy asked.

"You know, Starr, them quarters down by the town. We persuaded a few of 'em to move along."

"How'd you manage that, Jack?" Billy asked, remembering what Jessie had told him.

"Oh, we got our ways," Jack said, grinning.

Billy climbed off his horse and started toward the house. He nodded to the men who greeted him.

"Sure glad to have you back, Starr," they all said.

"Nice to meet you, Starr," a new hand said. "I'm Les Prewitt. I hear you're the fastest man around."

Billy shook hands and mumbled replies. But his feet continued their steady approach to the house.

"Well, look who's here," Mr. McNally said when Billy opened the door. "Jason, it's your old friend Billy Starr."

Jason McNally turned toward Billy and smiled. Jason seemed different, more of a man than a seventeen-year-old should have been. The boy's eyes were dark, brooding.

"Never got a chance to thank you for looking out for the boy," McNally said, shaking Billy's hand. "Saved his life like as not."

"Closer to th'other way around," Billy said. "I expect Jason here can take care of himself."

"Still, you did a job of work out there," McNally said. "We counted nine bodies altogether. How many you figure you shot?"

"Five or six anyway," Jason said. "I got one, and I think Wade Bennett might've nailed a couple."

"Call it an even half-dozen. That's three hundred dollars, a neat-enough bonus," McNally said, counting out the money.

"Keep it," Billy said, pushing the bills back at the rancher. "I did it for Wade. And 'cause they shot at me first."

"But you're still entitled – "

"Keep the money!" Billy shouted. "I don't need to be paid extra for doing a job and protecting my friends."

"However you want it, son," McNally said.

"I'm nobody's son," Billy said, trembling slightly. "I only came here to tell you I'm ready to go back to work."

"Well, Mike's out in the yards

somewhere," McNally said, a little shaken by Billy's outburst. "There's enough to be done to keep you occupied. See him. Jason, run out and locate Mike."

"I can find him," Billy said, retreating through the door.

It wasn't Dunstan, though, that Billy came across. It was John McNally. The young man wore a new silver-plated Colt on each hip. His gunbelt was studded with Mexican silver pieces.

"Just a minute there," John said, stepping in front of Billy.

"Got something to say?" Billy asked, frowning.

"Yeah," John said. "You're not needed here anymore. We've got all the men we need. Sure don't have any use for a busted-up old man."

"Your father didn't tell me you were running things now," Billy said, glaring at young John.

"Lots of things have changed since you got yourself shot. I'm top man now and I do the killing."

"You're not even full-grown," Billy said, shoving John aside.

"Nobody does that to me!" John screamed, firing a shot at Billy's feet.

A hush settled over the barnyard, and Billy turned slowly.

"You're not talking to my kid brother now," John said. "This McNally doesn't run scared 'cause an old man sneezes."

"Your brother's got twice the guts and three times the brains you have, John McNally," Billy said. "Any fool can shoot an unarmed farmer. "Two weeks ago you'd be dead if you'd shot a pistol at me."

"Two weeks changes lots of things," John said, smiling as his fingers tapped the twin pistols.

"Maybe," Billy said.

"I heard about how you'd gone soft on us, Starr. How you even went to church with that shopkeeper and her brother. Well, we don't hold church here."

"Maybe you should," Billy said, starting away again.

Once more the pistol fired and a plume of dust kicked up beside Billy's boot. When Billy failed to stop, John fired a third shot.

"I didn't come back here to stir up trouble," Billy said.

"Looks to me like that's just what you did," John said, laughing as he fired again.

"Señor Starr," Miguel called to Billy, racing across the yard with Billy's gunbelt.

"Now we'll get to it," John said, grinning broadly.

Billy took the gunbelt and slipped it around his waist. As he fastened the buckle, a hundred thoughts raced through his mind. He saw Jessie standing there, warning him to escape. But Billy saw no refuge, no way out.

"There's been enough killing out here," Billy said. "I didn't come back here to do more of it. If I'm not needed, I'll ride out."

"Gone soft, Starr?" John asked. "Soft in the guts?"

"Guess so," Billy said, glaring again at John McNally. "I have a little trouble keeping my stomach down when boys go shooting off their mouths."

"You heard what I said, Starr!" John shouted. "You're not wanted here anymore!"

"That's not exactly the way I see things," Dunstan said, appearing at last. "You think you're ready to take over, you try me, sonny boy. If Starr's got other things on his mind, well, I don't mind obliging you."

Dunstan's cold confidence unsettled the young man. For a minute, Billy thought it was all over. But the other men had gathered around, and young McNally wouldn't back down.

"You running, Starr?" John asked.

"I told you this was finished!" Dunstan yelled.

But one of the ranch hands pushed a rifle into Dunstan's back, and it was a personal matter between Billy and John McNally once more.

"Well, Starr?" John asked.

"I hope you're not too good," Billy said, motioning for the others to scatter. "I promised myself I'd do no more killing, not even of the likes of you. Now make your move. Let's get it over with."

Billy felt his wrists tremble. Part of him wanted to turn away, but he didn't. There was something in John's eyes. Billy had no interest in being shot in the back. His fingers grew still, and the old coldness returned to his own eyes. Jessie's words were set aside, and the terrible reality of living and dying returned.

John McNally drew swiftly, and his arrogant stance showed he expected to win the duel. But Billy's hand had pulled out the long-barreled Colt and fired before young McNally's pair of pistols were even level. John cried out in pain, firing one gun into the ground and dropping the second as the lead pellet smashed the bones and tendons of his right hand.

"Consider yourself lucky," Billy

said, walking over to examine the shattered hand. "You'd get yourself killed shooting off your mouth like that to anyone else."

A look of utter terror flooded John McNally's face.

"You could've killed me," John said, clutching his bloody hand. "They said the bleeding would slow you down."

"I wouldn't draw on a man unless I knew him inside out," Billy advised as he wrapped a handkerchief around John's hand. "Get Dunstan to teach you the tricks. Then maybe you'll be able to get yourself shot dead before you turn twenty-one."

"You could have taken care of that yourself."

"I'm tired of being the world's judge, deciding who's to live and who's to die," Billy said. "Let it find some other way to weed out the bad apples."

"You've gone soft on me, Starr," Dunstan said as Billy headed for the barn. "Shooting at a man's hand! He's quick enough to've shot you dead."

"I'm done with the killing," Billy announced.

"Not likely," Dunstan said, laughing. "It comes back to a man."

"I'm tired of being Billy Starr, Dunstan. I'm sick of death, of blood. I've done enough!"

"You're top gun here now. You can't just sit down and let yourself go to seed. The others'll think you've lost your touch. You'll have the tramps north of Santa Fe up here challenging you."

"I've fought my last battle," Billy said. "I want more out of life than a Colt revolver and a night alone on the cold hard ground."

"It was a mistake to take you to that girl," Dunstan said, spitting. "I should've taken the bullet out myself."

"That's right," Billy said. "But now it's done."

Dunstan kept a close watch on Billy those next few days. Billy was forever shadowed, if not by Miguel, then by one of the other hands who was paired off with him. Dunstan assigned jobs farther and farther from the strip of range that bounded the few remaining farms.

It suited Billy just fine. There was much work to be done, preparing horses for the roundup. It was good, honest labor. Simple to understand. And it built Billy's muscles back to their former selves and gave him back the endurance that would enable him to cope with whatever happened.

That Sunday Billy rode into town to attend church with Jessie and Doug. The farmers appeared less hostile, and one or two even smiled.

"We haven't seen many of Dunstan's men around lately," one woman commented.

"Busy getting ready for the cattle drive," Billy told her.

As he walked Jessie back to the mercantile, she leaned her head on his shoulder and smiled.

"You're trying, aren't you?" she asked.

"Doing my best, ma'am," Billy said.

"But you're still with Dunstan." Jessie sighed.

"Working for Mr. McNally."

"And shooting his sons full of holes."

"You heard about that, did you? I tried to step back. And I didn't kill him, Jessie. I might have a month ago."

"I suppose it's too early to expect miracles."

When Billy returned to the ranch, he found the bunkhouse deserted. Miguel fixed a supper of beef and beans for the two of them, and Billy ate quietly.

"Where'd everybody go?" Billy asked.

"I don't know, señor," Miguel said nervously.

"Tell me, Miguel."

"Señor Dunstan, he say to tell you they go to meet the cattle drive from Texas."

"Too early for that," Billy said.

"I know this," Miguel said, his eyes fixed on the ground. "I think maybe he has gone to visit the farms again."

"I think so too," Billy said, spooning the last of the dinner into his mouth.

"Señor, it is dangerous to ride out there."

"I'll be careful," Billy said, smiling at the boy.

"You will not tell them I said this to you?"

"I'm not planning to talk to them at all. You keep quiet about it, too. Dunstan would skin you for saying anything."

"I know, señor," Miguel said, fear flashing through his eyes.

Billy saddled Bluebonnet and rode off into the night. It wasn't difficult to pick up the trail left by Dunstan and the others. The tracks of twenty horses were hard to hide, even if there'd been a reason to conceal them.

Billy followed the trail past town through a clutter of small farms. Up ahead he spied several bright torches, and he slowed his horse. As he came closer, he heard shouts and outcries. Someone screamed, and children whimpered. Billy hid Bluebonnet behind a grove of oak trees and crept forward as if he were still scouting Union troops during the war.

Below him, Billy spotted a circle of mounted men. In the center stood two men Billy could identify in spite of the masks covering their faces. One was Mike Dunstan; the other was Mr. McNally. Three bedraggled men knelt before them. Two teenage boys, several women, and some small children were there as well.

"You had your warning!" McNally screamed at the farmers. "When Hall and the judge went down, you folks should've left."

"What right do you have to come out here and terrorize us?" one of the farmers asked. "We ain't hurt you. I occupy my time breaking sod, planting seed, and bringing in water from the creeks."

"You sent men against us first," Dunstan said. "You came down and shot men in the back, skulking over to our land like polecats. Now you wonder why we're here."

"My eldest, Bob, went with the others." A woman spoke up. "He took his chances, and we had to bury him. But none of us here had anything to do with it."

"Shame," Dunstan said, laughing. "Seems like you ought to've done something to merit what you're going to get tonight. Eh, boys?"

The men around the farmers laughed, and a couple of them fired pistols in the air. Some of the children started crying and their mothers pulled them to their sides.

Billy stared at the cruel eyes of Dunstan and the others. He spotted a little reluctance in young Jason's eyes, but the rest were willing, even eager, to kill. John McNally, bandaged hand and all, held a rifle on two small girls.

"We'll leave," one of the farmers finally said. "It's not right, but we'll go. Nothing's worth getting shot over."

"Probably not," Dunstan said, laughing. "Right, boys?"

Laughter echoed across the valley, and Billy frowned. Then Dunstan waved his arms in the air and the men leveled their guns at the farmers and opened fire.

"Oh, God, no," Billy mumbled, watching in horror the faces of the children and the women. He had little sympathy for the men. Men always died in war. But the small, limp bodies of the little ones tore at his insides like some great clawed creature.

The whole thing was over in a matter of seconds. It only took a minute to murder the whole bunch. Afterward, John McNally walked through the bodies, kicking each corpse to make sure all were dead. Billy fought to keep from vomiting as John fired his pistol into one of the farmer's heads.

"That's for my mother, you pig keeper!" John yelled, kicking the dead man.

When John was satisfied that they were all dead, the others split up and began riding back to the ranch. Some paused long enough to set fire to the farm buildings. One group stayed around to dig graves for the bodies. Billy trembled. He was filled with a mixture of fear and rage.

More death, he thought. More bloodshed. Was any place on earth worth so much of it?

He recalled what Jessie had said about Dunstan, about how families had been murdered. She'd been right about that. Billy now found himself allied to something ungodly, something too grotesque to be imagined.

For a long time he stood there, watching the flames dance in the moonlight. Then he caught sight of a small figure, a child creeping through the high grass to his right. Billy crawled over, but someone else got there first.

"Hey, what's this?" a man's voice called out.

"Please, don't hurt me," a high-pitched voice pleaded.

"It won't hurt much, sonny," the older voice said.

Billy quietly circled the man, then drew his pistol and clubbed him.

"Come on," Billy said, grabbing the

child's hand. "And be quiet."

Billy dragged the boy along as he raced to reach Bluebonnet.

"Don't hurt me," the boy begged.

"I'm not going to hurt anybody," Billy said, picking the boy up and carrying him to the horse. Billy mounted the animal, then pulled the child up behind him.

"They killed my ma," the boy said, clutching Billy's back. "Pa, too. Even Henry and Ruth."

"Life can be hard," Billy said, nudging Bluebonnet into a trot.

"I'll get 'em when I'm old enough," the boy swore between sobs.

"Doesn't do any good," Billy said. "Besides, someone'll get to 'em long before that. It's always that way with men like them."

The boy wasn't listening, though. Billy felt tears falling on his back, and the grip of the boy's small hands grew tighter.

"Won't be long now," Billy said, staring at the lamps burning in the window of the hotel.

"Where you takin' me?" the boy asked.

"Church," Billy answered. "All right with you?"

The boy relaxed his hold and pressed his head against Billy, who took it for an answer.

Billy left the little refugee with Reverend Simpson. The minister asked no questions, and Billy volunteered little.

"I'll tend the boy," the reverend said. "You say the others are all dead?"

Billy nodded.

"And you did nothing?" Reverend Simpson asked with wide eyes.

"I couldn't stop it. Maybe if I'd gotten there sooner. I don't know. I'd say this was just the beginning, though. If I was a farmer, I'd be bound for Colorado."

"These people have a right to stay. If there were fewer men around like you, it'd be safe for women and children here."

"Thank you, Reverend," Billy said, angrily turning away. "I noticed you weren't out there protecting those people tonight."

Billy didn't wait for a reply. He mounted his horse and raced out of town.

15

BILLY rode like fury to the ranch. Something was boiling up inside him, something that had to explode into speech, into a noise like the booming of a cannon. He galloped through the gate and up to the band of ranch hands, ignoring their laughter.

"Hey, Starr, have a bottle," one of them said, tossing the whiskey toward Billy.

"No, thanks," Billy said, smashing the bottle against the gate of the corral with enough force to keep them distant. He wondered how many bottles it took to convince a man that shooting down helpless women and children was part of his job.

"He didn't have to do that," one of the men grumbled. "Could've told us he'd been to town."

Billy rode on past them, then slid off his horse and left it, reins dangling, outside the bunkhouse. He stormed to the McNally house, climbed the steps, slung open the door, and charged inside.

"Where you been, Starr?" Dunstan asked, walking over to Billy's side. "We noticed you'd ridden off. You were gone when we got back."

"Why didn't you invite me to your little party tonight, Mike?" Billy asked, smiling in a way that hinted of violence.

"Didn't know you liked to drink that much," Dunstan said. "I'll get you a bottle."

"I meant the party you had south of town," Billy said angrily. "You know, the one where you roasted a few houses, planted some seeds, so to speak."

"What are you talking about?" Dunstan asked, trying to laugh away the comment.

"You know, Mike, plant. Put into the ground. Dig a hole and throw something in," Billy said, choking on the bitterness that flowed through him. "Do you suppose if you plant a little kid, it'll grow into a man?"

"I don't know what you're talking about," Dunstan said, nervously shaking his head.

"I mean, Mike, you and McNally rode out tonight and slaughtered helpless women and children. If you're forced to kill men, well, I understand that. War is that way. But kids – God, how could you stand there and shoot down all those little ones? I saw some that could hardly walk."

"You can't believe everything you hear in town," Dunstan said, taking a long sip of his whiskey.

"Can't I?" Billy asked.

"We didn't ride anywhere tonight," McNally said.

"Don't lie to me!" Billy said, throwing a chair across the room. "All a man has to do is glance into the corral to see the way the horses are lathered. I can see the blood on your boots, smell the death that's in this room. Don't you think I've got ears? I heard you! I saw every bit of it! You murdered those people!"

"You're just getting yourself all riled over something you don't know anything about," Dunstan said.

"It was a revenge raid," McNally explained. "We hit them because they killed my wife."

"How many times have you done it?" Billy asked.

"This was the third," Dunstan said.

"And the last," Billy announced with eyes that flashed fire.

"Not a chance of that," McNally said. "As long as one of those sod-busting sons of Satan are on my land, we'll be riding out to see them. They won't stay much longer, not after tonight."

"How can someone who shoots down little children call himself a man?" Billy asked. "What is it that chokes the goodness out of a person, makes him do such a thing? I know all about Dunstan. The Kiowa told me. But what you did tonight . . . it was like you did it for fun."

"A man should enjoy his craft, Starr," Dunstan said, refilling his glass.

"I feel dirty just being around you," Billy said, turning away.

"I didn't hear anybody give you permission to leave," John McNally said, blocking Billy's path.

Billy took the young man's hand, twisted it, and slung him against the wall. When John bounced off, Billy hit him in the face with such force that the boy crumpled into a ball and collapsed onto the floor.

"Don't touch me, you filthy swine!" Billy shouted. "And you two!" Billy added, drawing his pistol as quick and cool as a man could. "You come around me, I'll kill you. I mean to put the violence behind me, but I swear I'll shoot you dead if you ever ride out like this again."

"You need a drink, Starr," Dunstan said.

"I need to be sick," Billy said, knocking the bottle out of Dunstan's hand. "But more than that, I need to be out of here."

Billy stomped back out of the house and headed for the old corral. There he found Comanche stomping the ground. He led the powerful black horse around to the barn and left him beside Bluebonnet. Then he headed for the bunkhouse.

Billy marched inside, knocking aside people who got in his way. He ignored their grumbling, the angry shouts, and the insults. In order to reach his bunk, he had to step over two men who'd passed out on the floor. He pulled out the heavy war chest, grinding his teeth as pain from his shoulder flashed down his back.

"I been looking for you, señor," Miguel said. "I told Señor Dunstan you ride off. He know you follow him."

"I told him so myself," Billy said, the fury in his eyes frightening the Mexican boy.

"I'm sorry, señor," Miguel said, running off.

Billy kicked the bed and opened the trunk. Hurriedly he threw his scattered belongings inside, then closed the padlock securely.

"Going somewhere, Starr?" Dunstan asked from the opposite side of the room.

Several of the hands stumbled to their feet and stared. Dunstan almost never entered the bunkhouse. Some of them slipped out the side door and scattered. Others spilled out the back. A few leaned against the wall and smiled. Something was about to happen.

"What's it to you?" Billy asked, fastening the belts that reinforced the chest's sides.

"I put a lot of time into your training, Starr. You can't just walk out on me."

"Can't I?" Billy asked.

"No, you can't," Dunstan said, stepping nearer. "You owe me."

"I owe you nothing," Billy said, his mouth contorted into a kind of snarl.

"I made you what you are. You were nothing before I picked you up off the floor of that Dodge City saloon."

"I was a man then," Billy said. "I had some self-respect! Now what am I?"

"The fastest gun on the Cimarron. Why, there are those who'd pay you thousands of dollars to take a man out."

"How much could I get for shooting Mike Dunstan?" Billy asked. "Know any kids who'd pay me to finish off the murderer of their families?"

"You better cool off," Dunstan suggested.

"You just stand there and pray I don't blow up and shoot you down for the dog you are, Dunstan. You hope to high heaven I don't remember your face the way it was when you started the shooting tonight."

"I do a job, Starr. I hire out to whoever's paying."

"You'd just as soon be on the other side, right?"

"No, I never hire out to farmers. There's no future to that. Once they get the land, it's done for."

Billy picked up the shiny new Winchester beside his bed and set it on top of the trunk. Then he picked up the chest and groaned as he carried it out of the bunkhouse.

"Starr, I'm not finished with you!" Dunstan shouted.

"Yes, you are," Billy whispered, panting as the weight of the chest got to him.

"Let me give you a hand," Jason offered, taking one end of the trunk.

"You better stay out of this," Billy warned. "It's trouble."

"I do what I want," Jason said, helping Billy get the chest to where Comanche stood waiting.

"Like tonight?" Billy asked, his eyes catching fire again.

"After tonight," Jason said.

Billy spread a heavy saddle blanket across Comanche's back. Then the two of them lifted the old trunk onto the horse, and Billy lashed it into place.

"Starr, turn around!" Dunstan called out then.

Billy tied off the last rope, then turned so that his eyes met Dunstan's.

"Nobody rides away from my camp, Starr!" Dunstan yelled. "Nobody!"

"My back's easy enough to hit," Billy said. "Seems like you kind of like to do it that way."

"We're not finished with this thing. There's no two ways to life during a range war. You're either with me or against me."

"That'll be your choice," Billy said.

"No, yours. Ride out of here tonight, and you're a marked man. Bounty of a thousand dollars goes on your head."

"You do that, Dunstan, and I'll put the same figure on yours," Billy said, grinning. "And there are those who'd find you easier to take."

There was a stir among the men, and Dunstan frowned.

"You owe me!" Dunstan shouted.

"No, you owe me. It was me saved your neck from the Comanches. It was me took Luke Hall for you. Now, you listen. I don't plan to take a hand in this mess of yours. But if you mean to press things, go ahead. Let's have done with it."

Billy's eyes turned even colder than before, and fear appeared for the first time on Dunstan's face.

"You won't stay away, Starr," Dunstan said. "You're no different from me, from Hall and the rest. It's inside you, like right now. You'll kill again. And you'll do it at my bidding."

"Not likely," Billy said, leading Comanche out of the corral. "About as likely as finding ice water in hell."

Some of the men laughed, but Billy paid no attention. He climbed onto Bluebonnet's back and led Comanche along beside him. Soon they disappeared down the road to Cimarron City.

About a mile from town Billy detected the sound of a rider behind him. He slowed, then swung his pistol around to face the approaching rider.

"It's all right," said the slight figure,

emerging from the darkness. "It's me, Jason."

Billy allowed the young man to pull even with him, then started once more toward town.

"I'm not going back," Billy said.

"Didn't come to ask you," Jason explained. "I wanted to talk to you about tonight. I heard you telling off Pa."

"Talk to him," Billy said.

"I want to talk to you," Jason said, his speech a bit slurred from the effects of alcohol.

"You don't understand," Billy said, glaring at the boy. "I've done all the talking I want to do to you, your father, Dunstan, anybody!"

"Them!" Jason shouted. "They could care less about how I feel. They didn't get sick staring at all that blood. They didn't die watching those little kids stare at them."

"And now you're sorry, huh?"

"I never even fired my gun."

"But you didn't stop it, either," Billy

said. "It's all the same, you know. We were there."

"I won't be next time. I won't go."

"That changes everything, doesn't it?" Billy said, laughing. "There'll go on being a next time. And not being there won't help your conscience one bit."

"I can't call Pa on it. Or John, either. Most of all, not Dunstan. All I'd get is killed."

"Then let me tell you something, boy. You ride down this road until it takes you past the Cheyenne camps to Colorado. You climb up into the mountains and make a life for yourself. And don't ever look back."

"But my home . . . "

"You go back there, you'd best get accustomed to going along, joining in the shooting. Even a snake does its own biting."

"Is it hard hitting the trail alone?"

"Not with a clear head and no ghosts haunting you."

"Thanks, Billy," Jason said, kicking

the horse into a trot. “Is it pretty in Colorado?”

“Mountains block out the sun,” Billy said.

Young McNally spurred his horse, and Billy smiled as the boy rode westward.

“They say someone gets a fresh start every morning out here,” Billy told himself aloud. “I hope he’s not the only one.”

16

IT was well past midnight when Billy knocked lightly on the door of the mercantile. His first notion had been to take a room at the hotel, but he felt a need deep within himself to touch another human being. And there was only one person who would reach out to him, only one who would understand.

"Who's there?" called out a slightly hostile voice from inside the store.

"Billy Starr," Billy answered. "I need to speak to Jessie."

"She's asleep," said the voice, which Billy now recognized as Doug Hart's. "Go away."

"I'm not going," Billy said. "I have to see her."

"All right," Doug reluctantly agreed, opening the door. "Can't it wait for morning? It's been a long night already.

As you probably know."

"What?"

"Somebody brought in a little boy from one of the farms. Your friends shot his folks, even his little sister. A couple of other kids straggled over to Mrs. Hawkins's house. You had a real fine time tonight, didn't you?"

"Oh, I had a wonderful time," Billy said, fighting back the rage that was building up inside him. "Get Jessie."

"You're not welcome here."

"You made that clear. Get her!"

Doug disappeared upstairs. Some heated conversation followed. Then Jessie appeared, her shoulders draped by a heavy quilt. Her eyes flashed angrily.

"Douglas told you to go," she said. "There's not much to say. I've got a boy upstairs with Douglas who's too small to truly understand that he's got nobody now. Tomorrow we'll put him in a wagon bound for Dodge City. He's got some aunt in Abilene. Not much family when you're only ten years old."

"I left the ranch," Billy mumbled.

"You what?"

"I left the ranch."

"I can see that. You're here."

"You don't understand, Jessie," he said, trembling slightly. "I left for good. I saw it all. Dunstan didn't take me, but I followed them. God, it was pure murder. Shooting down women and kids!"

"I told you, Billy," she said, her face growing not a bit less hostile.

"And I said I'd have to see it for myself. Well, I have. I told Dunstan I wouldn't be back."

"Others have tried to leave," Jessie said. "Well, I'll fix you breakfast in the morning, and Douglas can help you tend your horses tonight. It's best you head for the mountains early."

"I'm not going to the mountains," Billy told her. "If I can find work, I'm staying here."

"Here?" she asked nervously. "That will never do. Dunstan will send men after you."

"He may have some difficulty doing

that. You forget. I'm the one with the reputation. No one around here's going to challenge Billy Starr."

"He's got a long arm, Billy," Jessie warned. "He won't want you here unless you're on his payroll, doing his bidding."

"That's too bad," Billy said, beginning to smile. "I'd hate to make him unhappy."

She returned his smile, and a certain brightness appeared in Billy's eyes.

"You've left it all behind?" Jessie asked. "The sadness and the hate?"

"I'm trying. It won't he easy."

"You're wearing a gray hat," she said, noticing the old, wrinkled Confederate hat in Billy's hand.

"My cavalry hat," Billy explained. "I don't even remember putting it on. I suppose I've had it with me all night."

"You're the one who brought little Tommy Reynolds in, aren't you?" she asked. "Reverend Simpson wouldn't say who it was. But he said it was a friend."

"That's the most praise he's directed my way lately."

"I'll have Douglas help with your horses," Jessie said, turning.

"Not just yet," Billy said. "Sit with me for a moment first."

"All right," she agreed.

They sat together and enjoyed the darkness. Nothing was said, but as Billy squeezed Jessie's soft hand, a tenderness was shared. Billy sighed. A special peace began to fill the emptiness inside his chest.

"You know, Jessie, everything's changed for me during the past few days," Billy told her. "For the first time since leaving home, I haven't missed Ellen."

"Oh?"

"I've missed you," he said, holding her closer.

"Have you got a place to stay?" she whispered.

"There are always rooms available at the hotel."

"Take the little room behind the

kitchen," she said. "Douglas sleeps there when we put somebody in the big room upstairs. I don't think he'd appreciate you staying upstairs with me."

"People talked enough when I was laid up with a bad shoulder. It'd be better with me at the hotel."

"People in this town can talk all they want," she said, her face growing a little red. "They have no business looking down their noses at anybody."

"It matters to your brother what people think of you," Billy told her. "And to me."

"I'll ask Douglas to help you get settled in. I'll make up your bed."

"Sure," Billy said, touching the softness of her cheek with his fingers.

Jessie crept back upstairs and brought her brother down. Doug was trying valiantly to tuck his nightshirt into a pair of overalls a bit too small for it all to fit in easily. Billy fought against grinning, but when the boy tripped over the bottom of the trousers, the three of them joined in an outburst of laughter.

"You'll get used to this if you stay long, Billy," Jessie said. "Douglas is only a fair runner, but he's about the best we've got at tripping over his own feet."

"He's staying?" Doug asked.

"For as long as he wants," Jessie told her brother.

"Where?" the boy asked angrily.

"Behind the kitchen," Billy said, "unless it bothers you, Doug. I could stay at the hotel."

The wrinkles on the boy's forehead faded, and he looked Billy dead in the eye.

"Tommy heard you talking," Doug said. "He says you're the one who brought him in. That right?"

"Surprise you?" Billy asked.

"More than a little. I'm sorry for what I said before." Doug extended a hand that nearly disappeared as Billy grasped it firmly.

"What would you say to helping me out with my gear?" Billy asked.

"That's why I came down," Doug

said, following Billy outside the house.

The two of them walked to Billy's horses. Together they untied the lashings that held the old war chest onto Comanche's back and dragged the trunk into the small cubicle behind the kitchen. Then Billy returned and stripped the saddle from Bluebonnet's back. When he was finished, Doug led the horses down the street to the stable.

"I'll brush 'em for you," Doug called back. "You likely have some things to say to Jessie."

"Thanks," Billy told the boy.

Billy hauled his saddle and the Winchester rifle inside the store. Jessie motioned to a small closet behind the counter. He stowed the gear, then continued on into the kitchen.

"How's the shoulder?" Jessie asked. "You're stooping."

"It ought to be fine," he told her.

She peeled back his shirt and frowned at the blood trickling from the wound.

"You'll kill yourself one of these

days, Billy. Wounds need time to heal properly. You could develop blood poisoning."

"It won't happen like that," he said, looking away from her. "No, I'll go quick, sudden. That's the way out here."

"Clerks in a mercantile usually die of boredom," she said, laughing.

"Is that what I am now?"

"Only part of the time. Is there any trade you know?"

"Besides horses? No, none that I can think of. I guess I could work with guns. I built this Colt," he told her, turning the pistol over in his hands.

"Well, there's market enough for ten gunsmiths in Cimarron City. It won't remind you too much of the other life?"

"Men do the killing. Guns don't," he told her.

During the next few days Billy found himself splitting time tending the counter of the mercantile and mending guns in a small shed he and Doug built behind the store. It was what the reverend called honest labor, and it swept Billy's mind away from the ghosts of other times, from the memories of dead men and weeping children.

Billy also practiced carpentry. He mended broken floorboards at the hotel and enlarged the small room behind the kitchen so that he had more living room. Young Tommy Reynolds was packed off to Dodge, and the mercantile was once more left to the three of them.

From time to time Billy would frown as farmers rode through town, their families and furniture piled in the back of ancient wagons. Some used haggard old mules to pull loads a team of six oxen couldn't have handled. It was a sad thing, knowing so many of them would fall prey to the long, hard trail to Colorado.

But even as some of the farmers left, others arrived. There was movement west out of Texas, and land along the Cimarron was free if a man could hold on to it.

Someone else appeared in town for the first time that week, a tall, dark-haired man with a thick black mustache. Haley, he was called. His eyes were burnt brown and filled with a kind of menace that Billy recognized immediately. Two bright, silver-plated pistols rested on his hips, and he walked with the swagger of a Mississippi riverboat gambler.

"I hear you've got a fast hand with a gun," Haley said to Billy one afternoon at the mercantile. "Likely we'll be meeting before long."

"Wouldn't count on it," Billy said. "There's no profit to it. Hasn't Dunstan told you? I'm retired."

"He said to tell you nobody quits his outfit. And I'm fast, Starr. Fast as lightning."

"And loud as thunder," Billy said, laughing.

For the most part Billy ignored Haley just as he ignored all the others from the ranch. But it was difficult to miss the hatred that filled John McNally's eyes, the anger that Dunstan showed.

"You didn't set yourself in high stead with old man McNally, either, Starr," Dunstan said to Billy one morning. "His boy Jason took off the same night you left."

"Couldn't take to shooting down little kids, I guess," Billy said. "I told him which road leads to Colorado."

"We'll be burying you before too long, Starr," Dunstan said, frowning.

"I guess you'll try," Billy said, concentrating on the revolver he was cleaning. "But it's likely to be a long time before you shovel any dirt over me."

Still, Haley hovered around town like a dark cloud over a fine Sunday afternoon. It wasn't possible to avoid the man altogether, but Billy tried his best. As a precaution, he kept his Colt handy. Then one afternoon there was a sound of something rattling around on the porch of the mercantile. Billy walked out to investigate.

What Billy witnessed ignited an old fire deep within him. His face filled with fury, and he glared as Haley kicked young Doug Hart in the ribs.

"Boy, you're downright clumsy," Haley said, knocking a pail of eggs from Doug's hands.

"Leave him be," Billy said, stepping between the boy and Haley.

"Sticking your nose in where it's not needed, eh, Starr?" Haley asked.

Billy drew back his right hand and flattened Haley with a single blow.

"You're going to pay for that," Haley said, struggling to his feet.

"You all right, Doug?" Billy asked, keeping his eyes glued on Haley's every movement.

"Sure," Doug said, shaking the dust from his trousers. "He ruined five dollars' worth of fresh eggs, though."

"Five dollars, Haley," Billy said, holding out his hand for the money.

"I'll see you in hell first, Starr," Haley said, grinning.

"You'll be there, sure enough," Billy said, smiling. "You'll have a long wait for me, though. Five dollars!"

Billy's face was scarlet. The veins in the back of his neck protruded.

"Here," Dunstan said, tossing a gold piece at Billy's feet. "That settles things, right?"

Billy kicked the coin over to Doug, who picked it up.

"Get inside," Billy told the boy.

"I'll fetch the rifle," Doug said.

"You'll go inside and leave me to do what I do best," Billy told him.

The boy reluctantly stepped inside the store. Billy walked out into the street and turned a half circle so that both Haley and Dunstan were in view.

"Well, Haley?" Billy asked.

"This isn't the time," Dunstan announced.

"Look, don't you worry, Mike," Haley said. "I can take him. He's soft from clerking."

"Nobody takes that man when his eyes are like that," Dunstan said, turning around. "Now come on."

"No!" Haley shouted.

"Go with old Mike there, Haley,"

Billy said, backing away. "I've killed enough men in my life."

"Look at him, Mike," Haley said. "He's running like a pup that stepped in a fire."

"Another time, Haley," Dunstan declared.

"Now's a good time for me," Haley said, moving so that the sun fell in Billy's eyes.

Before Dunstan could object again, Haley drew his gun. But Billy was as quick as ever. A single shot rang out, and Haley's head snapped back. A red blotch appeared over the newcomer's right eye and the gunman fell, dead.

Billy turned quickly toward Dunstan, but the man held his hands clear of his holster.

"You heard me, Starr," Dunstan said, his face growing pale as Billy stepped closer. "I told him not to draw."

"And you're not the one who's had him after me for a week, are you?" Billy asked. "You just didn't want him drawing when I was mad. You wanted me to face him when things were calm, and I wasn't expecting it. Well, Mike, that man couldn't have outdrawn me at a Sunday picnic. Now get out of here!"

Dunstan motioned for two ranch hands to remove Haley's body. Billy retreated to the mercantile and backed his way through the door. Once safely inside, he replaced the Colt in his holster.

"Billy?" Jessie called out, running to his side. "Thank God you're all right!"

"I'm not all right," Billy said. "I shot another man."

"I saw it," she told him. "Douglas told me what happened. You were taking up for him. You had to defend yourself."

"That's what I've told myself for a long time, Jessie. But it's all a lie. Defending myself? That's just what a man says who can't face the truth. I'm a killer, pure and simple. And no matter what I do, how far I run, it always comes back to me."

17

THE killing of Haley shook Billy out of his protected little world at the mercantile. He became a curiosity in Cimarron City, someone to be gawked at and spoken of in whispers. He felt the eyes of children and strangers on his back, heard his name mumbled by drunkards.

Boys who came to the mercantile to pick up yarn for their mothers or plow bits for their fathers would ask him how many men he'd killed or who was the fastest gun he'd ever seen. And each would later boast of how he'd talked to Billy Starr, the steel-eyed man who'd shot down Luke Hall in the parlor of the hotel and Haley in the street.

It was during this time that another stranger rode into town. That in itself was not unusual. Cimarron City was a town of strangers. But this man was different from the drifting saddle bums and penniless farmers who passed through on their way somewhere. Different, too, from the unshaven outlaws fleeing the laws of Kansas or Texas.

Doug told Billy the man called himself Jack Sawyer. It was an unfamiliar name to Billy, but there was nothing new about the man's look. He wore a long black coat over dark trousers and a white lace shirt. His polished Colt revolver hung loose on his right hip. The man's eager gray eyes held an expression that Billy'd seen too often in his own.

It wasn't long before Sawyer paid a visit to the mercantile. Billy had been cleaning a pair of Winchester rifles for a farmer named Bishop that morning, and Sawyer paid for the repairs and took the rifles.

"Heard you had some excitement out here a few weeks ago," Sawyer said. "Fire trouble."

"Not here," Billy told him.

"I heard it was a little ways outside town. Had to do with a disagreement over occupations."

"Speak your mind, mister," Billy said, putting his hands on the counter. "If you've got a thing to say, best say it."

"There's been killing of farmers in this territory," Sawyer said. "Murder, plain and simple."

"There's been killing on the open range by both sides."

"I understand you've done your share. How many is it now fifteen, twenty?"

"That's a little generous," Billy said, shaking his head. "No man's died at my hands who didn't merit it. I've gone looking for no trouble. And I've turned away from that path."

"They tell me over at the hotel that you're Billy Starr. You shoot a man name of Luke Hall?"

"I'm called that. And I killed Hall."

"We going to have trouble, Starr?" Sawyer asked. "They say you've got a quick hand."

"Let's hope you don't find out," Billy

said. "If these rifles are all you've come for, I hope you'll be on your way."

"I'm in no hurry," Sawyer said. "Tell me, Starr, what were you doing the night the farmers got themselves shot? I heard you rode the range for McNally."

"I patrolled the range, but I've never had much of a stomach for the kind of riding they do out there in the evening. I've no heart for shooting women and little kids."

"Got a soft spot, do you? Like for the Reynolds boy."

"Who?"

"Tommy Reynolds."

Billy scratched his head for a minute. Then he remembered. That was the farm boy he'd taken into town that night.

"Wasn't any trouble," Billy said. "Jessie Hart put him in a wagon bound for Dodge."

"I was thinking more about how you brought him into town. Was a rare-enough thing."

"Look, how did you learn all that?

Only two or three people in town know it was me, and they wouldn't tell you."

"Tommy told me," Sawyer said. "I'm his uncle."

"Then you rode down here to get even." Billy sighed. "That's what this whole mess is about, you know. Getting even. Well, it doesn't matter anymore. McNally lost his wife, so he'll kill every man, woman, and child on plowed land. And the farmers'll hire somebody like you to get rid of McNally and Dunstan. There's land enough for everyone here, but farmers tend to multiply themselves, carve up the range. There's need of open range through here, and there are those who'll die for it."

"And kill," Sawyer said.

"It's the same," Billy told him.

"I came to you because Tommy said if I needed a friend, I could count on you. I'm a U.S. marshal, authorized to make arrests in this territory and in the Indian nations."

"Why don't you take on something

simple, like bringing in the Dalton gang? You won't get McNally without a troop of cavalry."

"We could do it, the two of us."

"I have a job, mister," Billy said. "I have a chance here for a new start, for a different kind of life."

"A man who won't fight for the law doesn't have much of anything."

"Look, Sawyer, I've stuck my neck out enough for one lifetime. I fought four long years for the Southern Confederacy. I've spent another five years crisscrossing this country, trying to find out who I am. I won't pass the rest of my days backing up some carpetbagging kind of Union justice."

"You're going to have to choose, Billy Starr," Sawyer warned. "Sooner or later, Dunstan and McNally'll either take you back or find a man to kill you. Their type conducts business that way."

"There's always the mountains."

"You don't strike me as the running kind."

"I'm changing."

Sawyer's appearance in town altered everything for the ranchers. A kind of uneasy truce came about, and for the first time that anyone could remember, nights in Cimarron City were quiet. Then news arrived that herds of Texas longhorns were coming up the trail, eager to fatten themselves on Cimarron grass. And it appeared that the battle lines were forming again.

One morning Dunstan appeared in the doorway of the mercantile. Billy nodded to the man.

"Morning, Starr," Dunstan said.

"Morning, Mike," Billy replied.

"Hear you've had some talk with this Sawyer fellow?" Dunstan asked, obviously nervous.

"He did most of the talking," Billy said. "We've got a mutual friend."

"You didn't come with him to the ranch, though."

"I've got no more interest in shooting people, Mike," Billy said, frowning. "You can believe that."

"I've seen you, Starr," Dunstan said,

laughing. "It's inside you, just like Danby and all the other really good ones. You cut down Haley like he was a ten-year-old kid. And Haley was good."

"I'm good, too," Billy said. "But I want more than that."

"What do you want? I'll get it for you. A thousand a month? Done. A house of your own? We'll build it. All I want is – "

"To employ my gun from time to time," Billy said. "I know what you're after, but it's not what I want."

"You like this, working with other men's guns, selling needles and stick candy behind the counter of a mercantile?"

"Yes," Billy said. "And when the day's done, I can go to sleep and not wonder who might be creeping up to shoot me while I'm dozing."

"You've got the yellow streak, huh?"

"If you want to think that, go ahead."

"I told you before, Starr, there's no two ways about it. You're with me or against me. I need a man. If you won't come, I'll get someone else to take this Sawyer fellow. And when I've got him buried away, you'll be next on the list."

"Why waste the time, Mike?" Billy asked. "Go back to the ranch and shoot a kid or two. Maybe that'll make you feel better."

"You're going to cost me some money, Starr. But I think I'll enjoy watching them lower you into the ground."

"You know something, Mike?" Billy asked. "There's one good thing about you. You don't change much. It's dangerous to be so predictable."

"Well, that's my weakness," Dunstan said. "Yours is that big bleeding heart you've got. It'll get you killed."

"Everybody's got to die sooner or later. It's better to die for something or somebody than for a handful of gold."

"No, Starr, any kind of dying's the same."

As Dunstan left, Billy considered what the man had said. It had been no bluff. Dunstan would hire someone, the fastest gunman who could be located. And Billy wasn't as sharp as he'd once been. Maybe he'd slowed down enough to let himself be taken. A terrible chill wound its way through him.

Jessie noticed his nervousness. She suggested riding down to the river for a picnic, and Billy jumped at the idea. It was quiet along the banks of the Cimarron, though it seemed a long journey for a picnic. Billy knew of a small grove of oak trees that would provide shade in the midst of the springtime heat, and it was there that Jessie spread out a large blanket.

"There's something about getting away from a town, even a small one," Billy said. "The open sky, the freedom."

"It's hard to run a mercantile business without a town, though," Jessie said.

"There are other things to do besides run a store," Billy said. "Ranching, for instance."

"You miss it, don't you?" she asked.

"I miss the horses," Billy said.

"There's something about riding across the open range with the wind in your face, the sun on your bare shoulders. I don't think a man ever gets old out there."

"I thought you were happy at the store." Jessie sighed.

"I'm happy with you," Billy said. "The store doesn't mean anything. I think we could be happy together in the middle of a desert."

"Maybe," she said. "But I think I'd have to have a purpose, some kind of work."

"You're one of the builders," Billy told her. "Papa was a builder."

"Tell me about him."

"His father died when he was young, like Doug," Billy said, sighing. "I don't remember how young, but before he was fifteen, I'd say. Papa quit school and moved his mama and sisters to town. They worked in a store. When he was old enough, he joined the army to fight Indians. He came to the Brazos with a wife and baby."

"You?" Jessie asked.

"My older brother," Billy said, swallowing.

"And?"

"There was nothing there but Comanches," Billy said. "Not too friendly, either. Papa and a chief named Yellow Shirt fought a long time over that valley. Papa built and Yellow Shirt burned. Finally, after the old chief'd lost all his sons but one, he made peace. And Papa began building the ranch."

"You miss that place, don't you?" she asked.

"It's the only home I've ever known," Billy said sadly. "And since I've been gone, I feel lost. I don't belong anywhere. I promised Papa I'd build up the ranch, and I didn't do it. It's the only promise I've ever made that counted. And the only one I wasn't able to keep."

"Why did you want to come out here, Billy?" Jessie asked.

"It was your idea, remember?"

"Was it really? You've been pacing the store like a caged cougar since dawn. You had to get out and run some. What are you thinking about?"

"I was wondering how you'd feel about passing the spring in the Rockies," he told her. "There's a need for goods up there, too. The Indians are mostly peaceful in the high country, and there's gold and silver. Tons of it. I could build us a cabin, and there'd be just the two of us."

"And Douglas."

"And Doug," he agreed. "There'd be work enough for two men. There'd be excitement, adventure. Best of all there'd be peace. I could take a new name, forget about this mess on the Cimarron."

"You don't have to run away to do that," Jessie said.

"Yes, I do. Dunstan came to the store this morning. He put it to me straight. I help him or suffer the consequences. He'll bring in a fast gun, maybe a big name. And when that marshal's dead, I'll be next."

"Once you prove you're not interested in getting involved in this range war, he'll leave you alone."

"No, that's not his way. You told me yourself. Every single time I make some progress, escape the killing awhile, it comes back like a shadow after the sun rises. Jessie, the killing will come back if I stay."

"Only if you give in to it," she said.

"Would you rather I stand there and let them shoot me?"

"Of course not," she said, resting her head on his shoulder.

"You remember what it was like with Haley. The man deserved killing. But I'm worn out, tired of being the avenging angel of the Cimarron. Let them shoot each other."

"It's going to be all right," Jessie whispered in a soothing voice.

"I wish life was as easy for me as it is for you," Billy said, running his fingers through her long, satiny hair.

"So do I," she said.

They spread out the food and ate the simple dinner. Then Billy took a blanket out of the wagon and rolled it into a sort of long pillow. He lay down beside Jessie, and they watched the magnificent sunset reflect itself in the still waters of the Cimarron.

"When I look at something like this, I believe there's a God," Billy said.

"There is," Jessie said. "He brought you to me."

"But will He let me stay?" Billy asked, his forehead filling with creases.

"I won't let you go," Jessie said, clutching his side. "We belong together."

"I love you, Jessie Hart," Billy said, caressing her shoulder with his weathered hand.

"That's all that matters," she said, rolling over against him.

As they embraced in the dying light, Billy wished he had the power to stop that moment, to freeze it in an eternal state of the present. But two hours later they were plodding homeward through the darkness, and he was wondering when Dunstan's new hireling would arrive.

18

THREE days later the tall white horse Jack Sawyer had been riding returned to the stable without its rider. Reverend Simpson and two men from the hotel took a wagon out east of town and located the marshal's body. There was a single bullet hole in the lawman's chest.

After that Billy began wearing his pistol everywhere. He kept the loaded Winchester beside his bed at night. His eyes were a little wider, too. Nothing went unnoticed, especially the glimmer in Dunstan's eye when he walked into the mercantile two days later.

"What can I do for you, Mike?" Billy said.

"Reconsidered my offer?" Dunstan asked. "Oh, by the way, did you hear about Marshal Sawyer? Seems somebody helped him meet with an accident."

"Tell me. Did he have an even chance?"

"He had his chance," Dunstan said.

"Then why not in town?" Billy asked.

"Well, Starr, nobody likes it known he shot a federal marshal. Besides, I thought you'd like to find out for yourself who's come to the territory. An old friend of yours, so to speak."

"Why couldn't you just leave it be?" Billy asked, his eyes growing dark with sadness. "You know I'll have to kill him."

"If you can," Dunstan said, smiling wickedly. "Either way, I figure I'll have a top gun with me again. You suit this girl just fine, working in her store and keeping her company. But when the shooting starts, she'll scatter like a jackrabbit. I've seen her kind before."

"You just can't stand for anyone to have a chance at something better, can you?" Billy asked.

"I told you, Starr. You owe me! I don't let a man forget his debts. Not ever!"

"Let me tell you something, Mike," Billy said, the anger returning to his eyes. "If you spoil this for me, I'll do what I can to make sure you lose something, too. I'm that way, you see. And I have a good memory. You'd best make sure your man is real good."

"He is," Dunstan said, smiling. "The best there is."

When Dunstan left, Billy took out his revolver and cleaned it for the third time that week. He oiled the cylinders until they twirled silently. He rubbed hot fat into his holster so that the leather was slick and smooth. He wanted every possible advantage. He couldn't forget the arrogant look in Dunstan's eye. It told of absolute confidence.

Billy wanted to explain it all to Jessie, but she was out of reach. She simply refused to hear anything that threatened the happiness they'd found. Strangely enough, it was young Doug who saw what was happening, who noticed the hardness returning to Billy.

One afternoon, as they were fishing for catfish in a creek, Doug said it all.

"Who's the man you're getting ready to kill, Billy?" the boy asked.

"I don't know," Billy said. "Haven't seen him."

"He won't show up until he's ready, will he? I've seen the way Dunstan looks at you. It took a fast gun to shoot Marshal Sawyer, too. I watched him shoot bottles one afternoon. He was quick."

"Quicker than me?" Billy asked, wiping sweat from his forehead.

"Maybe," Doug said. "Close, anyway."

They turned their attention back to the fishing poles for a time. Then Billy frowned.

"It's not how I want it to be, you know," Billy said. "I asked Jessie to go to Colorado with me."

"Would it be different there?" Doug asked.

"I think it could be. There's no chance of avoiding it here in Cimarron City. Too close to Dunstan. Once that man's made his mind up about a thing, it's bound to happen."

"No way out?"

"Not that I know of. I'll try. I really will. God, I don't want this to happen. I've come close to being happy here, Doug. Jessie's the first person I've let get to know me in a long time. Years. I care for her."

"I know." Doug sighed. "But it comes down to the same thing. You're going to hurt her."

"I told her what I was."

"She doesn't understand certain things, Billy," Doug said, gazing at him with an unexpected look of sympathy. "Like why you have to stand up to Dunstan. She can't see you're looking out for us, too. If there was law here, maybe you could stay, work in the store, and be left alone. But not the way things are."

"What do you think I should do?" Billy asked.

"Hey, I'm just a kid. I don't even know what to do myself. But I guess if it was me, I'd stay and have it out with them. If you start running, when do you stop?"

"Dunstan's so confident. I don't know who he's brought in, but it must be a top man. I could get myself killed real easy."

"Afraid?"

"Of dying? Maybe. Mostly of being adrift again. Dying, well, I guess I've thought about it before. Might be better than living this kind of a life."

"She really does love you, for what it's worth," Doug told him. "Is there something I can do?"

"Take care of her after I'm gone."

Billy never discussed with Jessie the words he'd shared with her brother. And he knew Doug would keep silent as well. If Billy'd become the gunman named Starr again in reality, in his heart he still hoped there might be a little time left for him as Billy Starr, gunsmith and mercantile clerk.

For a time it seemed as though Dunstan might have reconsidered. The cattle herds kept the ranch hands busy, and Dunstan himself hadn't been to town in days. But that all changed on Sunday afternoon at a big church supper down by the river.

There were many strangers there, and Billy took no particular note of any of them. Some were cowboys from Texas, and he talked with them about life along the Brazos, of the carpetbagger taxes and the hardships along the trail.

Billy was tossing horseshoes with Doug when the air seemed to grow still. A strange sensation prickled his spine. He turned his eyes and observed two men of medium height fifteen feet or so away. Doug put his second shoe a little more than three inches from the spike, but Billy gave the strangers a hard glance and slung the heavy iron shoe so low that it made a tremendous clank when it rolled around the pole and held on for a ringer.

"Good shot, Starr," the man on the right said. "Got a good eye for horseshoes. Know how to use a gun?"

"Some say so," Billy said, examining the newcomers. The first was a flashy dresser, decked out in white trousers, with a vest and a brown leather jacket. The other was wearing the ordinary garb of a cowboy: denim pants and a plaid shirt, dusty boots with big Mexican spurs.

"Billy?" Doug asked, walking over to retrieve the horseshoes.

Billy spread his legs slightly and motioned with his head for Doug to back away.

"I could use some target practice," the second man said, staring at Billy with hatred in his eyes. "Fast work for me."

"I don't need the exercise," Billy said, pulling Doug around behind him.

"Got a protective nature to him, Harry," the second man said. "Hear he's real cozy with a particular lady in that town. Goes to church with her. Even sleeps in the same house."

"You be quiet about my sister!" Doug yelled, fighting to get free of Billy's grasp.

"Don't you want to do something about that, Starr?" the man continued. "I'd like to do a little something myself to that gal. She's real friendly to strangers, I hear."

"I've got no interest in killing the likes of you," Billy said, backing away.

"How about you, then, little brother?" the man asked, laughing. "Harry, get this young man a gun."

The flashy dresser tossed a pistol at Doug's feet, but Billy kicked the gun away before Doug could pick it up.

"Go back and tell Dunstan it won't work," Billy said. "I won't oblige you today."

"This isn't for Dunstan," the cowboy said. "This is purely for me. You got a nature in you, Starr. You want to protect this here little boy. Like a brother to you, ain't he?"

"Yes," Billy said.

"Well, I know all about little brothers. I had one myself. He had a way of jumping into water over his head. I'd usually be around to pull him out. Then this fellow came to town, cheated the boy at cards, and shot him for calling the deal."

Billy frowned as it dawned on him. The flashy dresser was Harry Courtney And the talker, the one with the hard eyes? That was Texas Bob Smith.

"I remember," Billy said. "You're Smith. And Courtney. I thought there was another one."

"Got himself shot last month," Courtney said.

"Looks like neither of you takes too good care of your brothers," Billy said.

"We'll make this a joint project, Bob," Courtney said.

"Fine with me," Billy said. "Makes no difference. But you've been listening to the wrong man, Smith. Your brother called the gunplay. He was the one doing the cheating."

"Then how come you took off?" Smith asked.

"I didn't," Billy told them. "Dunstan knocked me over the head and hauled me to the stable. I wasn't afraid of you then, and I'm not now. But I've had enough of killing. I'm trying to start over."

"That's no easy thing for a man to do, Starr," Smith said.

"I'm only telling you how it was for me, Smith. If you force this, make me come out after you, then I'll kill the both of you. Dunstan, too. I'll paint this country red with your blood. You steal this chance from me, you'll pay."

"Will we, now?" Smith asked, laughing. "I tell you what, Starr. I hear you've gotten a little rusty. I don't figure even Luke Hall could have taken me and Harry both on the same throw of the dice. I guess maybe you're all talk."

"You think it's worth dying to find out, you try me," Billy said. "But I'd give it some thought. Come on, Doug. Let's find Jessie."

Billy walked away, ignoring the jeers of the men behind him. Smith taunted, said things that heated Billy's blood. But he fought it all off, trying to leave the killing behind.

"Who'd've thought it," one of the farmers said. "Old Starr got himself a pair of weak knees."

There was laughter, and Billy's face flashed red with rage. Still, he fought the urge to turn and force a showdown.

"I'm proud of you for what you did tonight," Jessie said as they rode home. "It takes a lot of courage to walk away from a fight. I'm glad it's over."

"Over?" Billy asked, his eyes alive with disbelief. "It's not over. This is only the beginning. And you'd better understand, Jessie. They won't come for me. They'll go after you and Doug."

"Douglas?" she asked, her hands trembling.

"It's Dunstan's way. You find a man's weakness, then go after it. They can't get to me on my own. But they know how I stick to you, how I took up for Doug before."

"I'm not worried," Doug said. "I can stay close to the store, and Billy can teach me to shoot."

"Teach you?" Jessie gasped. "I don't want him shooting anybody, and he knows it. I certainly won't have you waving a gun around, too, getting yourself shot to pieces."

"You can't keep his feet nailed to the floor, Jessie," Billy said. "Sooner or later, a man's got to learn how to defend himself."

"Even if it kills him?" she asked.

"Even then," Billy said. "It's hard out here, but you better understand something. To stay means Doug's got to learn to shoot, to take care of himself. Now in Colorado . . . "

"We've already discussed that," Jessie said.

"If we stay, Jessie," Billy said, his face growing deadly serious, "there's going to be more dying. Maybe me, maybe Doug. You talk about turning away from this like it can be done. It can't! Jessie, it's for you to decide. I'll try it your way. And Doug, he'd die for you. But it's all so unnecessary."

"I won't go running off to the

mountains, Billy Starr!" Jessie shouted. "I've worked too hard for what I have."

Billy looked back into Doug's anxious eyes and shared his concern. But then he felt Jessie's head on his shoulder and sighed. What would come must come. It was a thing he'd heard as a boy in the camp of the Comanches. In Billy's quarter century of living, he'd found it always to be true.

19

WHAT mainly came was Texas Bob Smith. Most of the day Smith would sit on a bench in front of the hotel and stare across the street at the mercantile. He'd sit there, whittling and humming some crude tune, laughing to himself as he waited for Billy to accept the challenge.

Occasionally Smith would walk across to the store, usually when Billy was busy in back. The gunman would whisper things about Jessie to Douglas, telling the boy things no brother could ever bear to hear about his sister.

"Liar!" Billy would hear Doug shout. "You pig!"

But Smith would always vanish before Billy could reach the front room.

"I'll kill him if you don't," Doug said

one morning. "He's no better than an animal."

We're all that way, Billy thought.

Smith appeared twice daily afterward to shout his challenge.

"Whenever you're ready, Starr!" Smith would shout. "Harry's waiting at the hotel!"

Billy would walk to the door of the mercantile and spit in the street.

"Why can't you leave us alone?" Billy would ask.

"It'd ruin the sport," Smith said. "We'll be around. Maybe next time we'll find that gal of yours by her lonesome. My, my, I could do with a little of that."

Billy felt his blood boiling, but he held back. As the hours and days grew into a week, though, he wondered if he could hold on.

"Sooner or later you'll come out and meet us, Starr," Smith said. "Sooner or later."

That night, as Doug started to close the store, Smith and Courtney barged into the place and kicked over a table of canned goods.

"Seems a bit early to be shutting things up, boy," Courtney said.

"We always close at sundown," Doug said, nervously tapping the counter.

"Your sister around, boy?" Smith asked. "She live in this dump?"

"Jessie's in back," Doug told them. "We live upstairs, but Billy's just back of the kitchen."

"Likely he's busy at the moment, huh?" Smith said, winking at the boy.

"Say, Bob," Courtney said. "You know, a gal pretty as she is ought to have a room over at the hotel. Ground floor. No, I got a better notion. She could stay upstairs with me. A few weeks of being around these boys, she ought to be ready for some real men."

Smith laughed. "You go get her," he said. "Tell her I've got room in my quarters for her. I don't figure she'll take up much space."

The two men laughed, and Doug glared at them.

"You foul-mouthed fools," the boy said. "You're not fit company for a hog!"

"Here, boy, do it like a man," Courtney said, taking a pistol from a shelf, loading it, and sliding it down the counter to Doug. "Pick it up and bark for us, pup!"

"We're closed, gentlemen," Billy said, stepping through the door in time to snatch the pistol from Doug's youthful hand. "Get out!"

"Why don't you just help us do that, Starr!" Smith shouted, backing up to give himself room to draw.

"Don't know as it'd be a fair fight," Billy said. "I see you mostly like to call out little boys and pick on women. Now get out of here!"

"Make us," Courtney said, squaring off.

Billy made a half turn, then swung his fist around so that it connected with Courtney's jaw below the right eye. The man stumbled, and Billy drove a shoulder hard into Smith's midsection, knocking both men through the door and on into the street.

"You'll pay for this come tomorrow, Starr," Smith said, angrily rubbing his ribs.

"I mean to see you dead," Courtney said, getting to his feet.

"You stay out of my way, hear!" Billy shouted.

"Oh, we'll be around, Starr," Smith said. "You can count on that."

Billy rubbed the tender knuckles of his right hand, then backed into the store and turned to Doug.

"Don't you ever pick up a gun like that," Billy said. "Nine times out of ten there wouldn't even be a ball in the first cylinder. They'd have shot you dead."

"I couldn't just let them keep saying those things about my sister," Doug explained.

"You think they'd stop after you were dead? Don't be stupid, Doug. This whole business has nothing to do with you. It's me they're after."

"Then settle it, Billy," Doug said, his eyes pleading for relief from the taunts of Smith and Courtney. "I can't stand this."

"You know how Jessie feels about it," Billy said. "If I have it out with them, she'll never forgive me. No, I've got to be strong enough to outlast them. They won't wait here forever."

"How long? A month? A year? You know when the last time I got to school was?"

"I'll walk you there from now on."

"And who'll watch Jessie while we're gone? Who's going to protect me when I'm in class? Teach me to shoot. That way I can protect myself."

"Jessie would kill me."

"To tell you the truth, Billy, I don't know if dying's a whole lot worse than this," Doug said, sinking into a chair. "I'm scared all the time. I keep expecting those two to charge in here and start shooting. What if they never go away?"

"I don't know," Billy said, squeezing

the boy's shoulder as a father might have done.

Billy returned to his work in the back then. He'd been caulking the kitchen windows and didn't finish till Jessie had dinner ready.

"More trouble today?" she asked Doug as the boy played with his stew. "You know better than to pay any attention to those men."

"I wish you'd let Billy take care of them," Doug said, setting down his fork and staring into her eyes. "He could do it."

"We'll wait for law and order to come to this land," Jessie told them both. "Won't be so very much longer."

"Sure," Billy said, sighing. "We had a marshal shot here, so they'll rush right off and send another. Don't deceive yourself, Jessie."

"It's still the way," she said.

"Maybe in Virginia, but not here. Before long they'll shoot one of you two," Billy said, glancing at the floor. "I can't let that happen."

He sat frozen for a long time, trembling as he envisioned what must be done.

"Come, sit with me in the front room for a while," Jessie said to him after it was clear that no one would eat any more. "Let the anger fade."

"That's not likely to happen," Billy said as they went into the parlor.

How could anyone so gentle have been born into this world? he wondered. She was like the little house his brother James had built near the river. The first strong wind always blew it into tatters. He wanted to protect her, to shield her from the violence. But how could he do it without losing her?

Around midnight Billy was awakened by the sound of gunfire. He pulled on his trousers, grabbed the Winchester, and made his way through the kitchen into the store.

Doug had beaten him there. The boy screamed something outside, then ducked behind the counter as a bullet shattered the window. Billy frowned as he observed the boy's trembling shoulders. Doug's knobby knees protruded from under his nightshirt, and Billy realized just how small the boy really was.

"Get down," Billy whispered as another shot smashed the window.

"It's them again," Doug said. "Smith and Courtney."

"You hear me, Starr!" Smith shouted. "How do you like our little visit? Sorry we were too late for dinner."

There was the infuriating laughter again, followed by a cascade of shooting. Bullets whined through the air, smashing shelves, knocking fixtures from the wall, showering them with glass. Two more shots barked out, and a cry split the air.

"I must've hit one of 'em," Courtney said. "I heard a yelp."

The two men laughed, but Billy fired the rifle twice and their horses shied away. As the riders fought for control, Billy scooped up Douglas Hart's limp figure and carried him into the kitchen.

Billy lit a small candle so that he could examine the boy more carefully. Aside from a handful of cuts caused by glass fragments, there was a larger wound in Doug's left forearm.

"Jessie, get in here!" Billy yelled as he pressed a cloth against the wound to stop the bleeding.

Jessie made her way into the room. She shook the slumber from her eyes and stared at the still form of her brother. A shiver wound its way through her body.

"Get hold of yourself," Billy told her. "When he comes to, he's going to need you. It's not so bad, but he's going to be pretty scared."

Jessie made a tourniquet from a strip of Doug's sleeping gown. As she wound it around her brother's arm, Billy released the pressure he'd been applying.

"The bullet went clean through," Jessie announced as she dabbed alcohol on the similar scars on the front and back of Doug's arm. "I'll get it bandaged. You wait in back. Don't do anything rash, Billy. He's going to be just fine."

"Can't you see what you've let me do?" Billy asked with probing eyes. "Your brother's lying there shot. He could as easily be dead. Your store's all shot to pieces. The front window's blown apart, and goods are lying all over the place."

"We can put it right again."

"Can you get another brother? It might be you next time!"

"Don't get all riled," she warned.

Billy turned and walked back into the store. Courtney and Smith were still out front, laughing and making their crude taunts. Billy slid through the door and fired his pistol twice rapidly, missing each man in turn by little more than an inch.

"You'd be dead right now if I had my way!" Billy yelled at them. "I've seen how well you do against little boys. Now you've got a choice. Be here at sunrise, and I'll shoot you down for the dogs you are. Or ride out of this country fast and hard. Understand?"

"Never asked for anything more, Starr," Smith said, leaning down from his horse and flashing a cruel smile. "We'll be waiting for you."

"Say your prayers, too," Billy told them. "Get ready to die!"

Billy shook with fury. When he got back inside the store, he said nothing to Jessie. He glanced at her brother, making sure Doug had regained his senses and wasn't still unconscious. Then he sat down and rammed a powder cartridge into one of the empty chambers in his pistol. He rolled a lead ball in afterward and fixed the needed percussion cap.

"Billy, you're not planning to face those men tonight!" Jessie cried.

"No," Billy told her.

"Thank heavens. You'll see. Everything will be better in the morning. When they see you won't face them, they'll leave."

"They'll never leave this town," Billy said coldly. "Somebody'll dig their graves here."

"But you said – "

"Jessie, I've been trying to explain myself to you. I won't stand by and let anybody be shot at by the likes of that pair. That makes me a violent man, I suppose. But this is a violent country. Sometimes a man has to take a stand, and a woman has to back him up."

"I know all there is to know about taking stands," Jessie said. "I lost a brother and a grandfather in the war. For nothing. I've watched this town, Billy Starr. You're not the only one with a conscience, but it never helps. If you kill those two, Dunstan will only send for three next time. Sooner or later, they'll kill you."

"Then go with me to Colorado."

"Before or after you kill Smith and Courtney?"

"There's paying to be done," Billy said, nodding to Doug.

"He's my brother, not yours," she said. "He didn't ask you to shoot them for him."

"Didn't he?" Billy asked with wide eyes. "More than once, too. He knows, Jessie."

She walked away, leaving Billy to face the tired eyes of young Doug.

When morning came, Jessie was surprised to discover Billy still sitting at the table, holding Doug's hand. Billy had felt no sleep coming. He was drawn to Doug by memories of another young man lying wounded in a faraway place nine years before, one named Willie Delamer.

"Have you been here all night?" Jessie asked.

"Doug sat up with me some," Billy told her.

"He's not hurt badly," she explained. "He'll be up and around soon as I get a sling made. He'll show that arm off to every other boy in the territory."

"That right, Doug?" Billy asked.

"Sure," the boy said, his speech slurred some by the whiskey Billy had fed him to lessen the pain.

"A drunk brother," Jessie said, smiling.

"You take care of him, Jessie," Billy said, rising from the chair. "I've got things to attend to."

"Don't go looking for trouble, Billy," she urged.

"I never have to look for it," he told her. "It has a way of finding me on its own."

"You're not going, are you?"

"I told you last night. It's the only way to put an end to it."

"Billy, listen to me," she said with a hard, cold look in her eyes. "If you go out there and shoot at those men, don't bother to return. You won't be welcome."

"Jessie?" Doug cried out from the table.

"I mean it, Billy," she said. "Don't come back."

Billy stared at her long and hard.

"If I stayed and did nothing, I wouldn't be me, Jessie," he told her. "I've never lied about myself, not to you, not to anyone. I am what I am!"

"You could change," she told him again. "People can always change."

"I don't think so." Billy sighed. "I tried. But I could never just watch what those men did to Doug without raising my hand. I guess that's the difference between us, Jessie. I'm sorry."

"I don't want you to be sorry," she said. "I want you to be here. If you go, it's going to be like Ellen all over again."

Billy's face grew pale, and his knees began to shake.

"You're probably right," he admitted. "But this is your doing, not mine. If something happens, I wrote two letters. One's for my sister in Colorado. The other's for my younger brother down in Texas. Please send the chest along to him."

"Billy?" she called.

But he didn't stop. He patted Doug on the knee, then buckled on his gunbelt. Moments later, Billy Starr stepped out into the street, ready to fight his final battle.

20

BILLY expected the street to be deserted. He took no pleasure in what was about to happen, and it was beyond his imagination that anyone else would. To his surprise, he saw both sides of the street crowded with people, ranch hands and Texas drovers on one side, farmers and their families on the other.

I hope they get their money's worth, Billy thought to himself. A bitterness swelled up inside him as he looked at the faces of the women and children. Men he'd once ridden beside stood smiling. Billy wondered if anyone on that street hoped he'd be alive to watch the sunset.

It was like the times he'd stood naked on the cliff overlooking the Brazos. Then, though, he'd touched the strange spiritual power of the place. Now he was utterly alone, left to search his soul for some kind of inner strength. He sought some meaning in what appeared to be a meaningless event.

He found himself recalling things once thought forgotten. He saw his father's proud face the year they'd first gone hunting together. He remembered that same face, older and pale, shortly before the surgeon had pronounced him dead after the first day's fighting at Shiloh.

There was Ellen, too. He recalled how light his legs had been when he'd chased her through the shallows of the river. How old had they been? Ten? Eleven? Had he ever been that young?

There was Wade Bennett, too. Wade should have grown old in McLennan County, surrounded by grandchildren who would listen to stories of the wild old days roping horses on the Cimarron.

The memories faded, swept away by the cold, cruel hand of reality. Billy watched Texas Bob Smith approach from the east, calling out the last challenge in his deep voice.

"Ready to get it done, Starr?" Smith's voice boomed out.

"I'm at your disposal," Billy said, circling to his right so that the sun didn't strike his eyes.

Smith stepped to the center of the street. Harry Courtney joined him. Billy waited for Dunstan to come out, too, but the man stayed cautiously beside the twin doors of the Gilded Saddle Saloon.

Billy took his stance beside an abandoned freight wagon. His hands felt tight, his fingers stiff. But as he stared at Dunstan, the anger bubbled up inside. Billy's eyes flashed cold and violent.

"When this is finished, I'll be on over to settle with you, Mike," Billy called out.

Dunstan just smiled.

"You people better get yourselves back some," Billy warned. "I'd hate to see anybody innocent get themselves shot by accident."

Billy said it so that the bitterness in his heart was apparent to all of them. Few sought the shelter of the hotel, though. Billy took a deep breath and sighed. His fingers relaxed. He fixed his eyes on the two men before him. He was ready.

"Nobody ever took Texas Bob Smith," Smith began. "But I guess maybe old Harry would like a try at you, too."

"You work it any way you want," Billy told them. "I'll do my part to put you both into the ground."

A silence settled over the street. Billy waited. His reflexes were sharp. His mind was clear. He'd done everything possible to prepare himself. There was nothing to look ahead to, nowhere to return. In that instant of realization, Billy Starr became the most dangerous man on the street.

With two men facing him, Billy should have drawn first. But he also needed to know which target to select first. He'd have just a split second to decide. He prayed his timing would carry him through.

First Smith, Billy decided. He's the quick one, or so the word had it. Courtney will be watching, not reacting. Once you do it, you have to move, and move fast.

An inner voice whispered to Billy, too. Watch Dunstan. Don't let anyone get behind you.

"Tell me something, Starr," Smith said. "Did my brother die quick?"

"Before he hit the floor," Billy said. "He was fast enough that I had to shoot to kill."

"I always aim to kill," Smith said, laughing. "Don't have to do a job twice that way. You know, when I finish with you, I just might take a turn at that lady across the street."

"You wouldn't get along with her," Billy said. "She doesn't take to guns."

"Wasn't planning on asking her about it," Smith said. "Wouldn't take but a minute or so to convince her to cooperate."

Billy just smiled. He bent his knees slightly. Smith started to say something, then reached for his pistol. Billy's hand flashed his Colt out like lightning, and the bullets fired at nearly the same instant.

Smith's gun was not quite level, though, and the bullet struck Billy's left foot. Pain shot through his leg, but there was no time to cry out. He rolled under the wagon as Courtney fired.

"Bob?" Courtney shouted, staring into Smith's lifeless eyes as the Texan buckled and fell. Billy's shot had struck Smith's head just below the left eye so that the entire rear of his skull was blown apart. Courtney went wild.

Bullets sprayed the ground in front of the wagon, and Billy fought to drag his dead left foot around so that he could get a clear shot at the other gunman. People were screaming and scurrying for refuge as Courtney retreated to the safety of a water tank to reload.

"I'm coming for you, Starr!" Courtney screamed, charging out onto the street.

Billy said nothing, just rolled past the front wheels of the wagon and fired twice, striking Courtney first in the shoulder and then in the neck. The man fell to his knees, staring with surprised eyes at Billy as death came.

"Can't be!" someone shouted.

But the two gunmen lay still, and the smell of death hung over the street, mingling with the heavy smoke left by the pistol fire.

"Dunstan!" Billy hollered, limping out onto the street. "Come and get yours!"

A ranch hand swung a rifle in Billy's direction and was rewarded with a shot through the head.

"Come on, Mike!" Billy yelled. "You wanted it this way!"

Billy limped on, feeling his boot grow soft and mushy as the bleeding worsened.

"No more, Starr," Dunstan said, stumbling along the side of the saloon. "It's done."

"Nothing's over till the man at the top goes down," Billy said, his eyes wild with rage.

"Look, Starr, you're welcome back at the ranch. McNally will pay you, pay you anything. What do you want? Two thousand? Five?"

"What do I want?" Billy said, choking. "I want . . . YOU!"

Dunstan's hand moved to his pistol, but Billy blew the holster from the man's belt. Billy then pointed his Colt at Dunstan's foot and fired.

"How does it feel, Mike?" Billy asked as Dunstan screamed out in pain. "How does pain hit you, Mike? Make you feel like the big boss of the ranch? Make you feel like you run this whole valley?"

"Starr," Dunstan begged, his face contorted in pain.

Billy raised his pistol and aimed it at Dunstan's face.

"Please, Starr, no!" Dunstan pleaded.

"On your knees!" Billy shouted.

Dunstan sank to his knees and gazed up at Billy's face. Tears appeared in Dunstan's eyes. Behind him the crowd stirred. Men who would have sold their souls to Mike Dunstan shook their heads and spit on the ground.

"Beg!" Billy yelled.

"I am begging you, Starr. I'm sorry."

Billy leveled the pistol and balanced it so that the barrel was in perfect alignment with Dunstan's head.

"Please!" Dunstan screamed.

Billy pressed the trigger.

The crowd stared as Dunstan's eyes closed, then reopened. A wicked smile spread across Billy's face. The hammer fell harmlessly. All six chambers had been fired. The gun was empty. "You knew?" Dunstan said, struggling to his feet.

"Did I?" Billy asked, his eyes as cold as steel.

Dunstan shuddered. He limped toward the hotel and yelled for help. The crowd melted away, and Billy made his way back to the store.

Always it comes back to me, Billy thought as he passed the bodies of Smith and Courtney. Always.

Billy turned the handle of the door and leaned against the frame.

"Dunstan!" Billy yelled.

The man turned back as Billy reloaded his revolver.

"Dunstan, you'd best keep to your side of the street from now on!" Billy shouted. "Next time we cross paths, I'll kill you!"

"I'll keep clear," Dunstan said, his eyes still clouded with fear.

"I hope so," Billy mumbled as he dragged his bloody foot into the mercantile and collapsed into a chair.

"Billy?" Doug called to him from behind the counter.

"Might be," Billy said, pulling off the blood-soaked boot and examining the wound.

"Is it all over?" Doug asked, walking slowly to Billy's side. The boy's face remained pale, and his injured arm was held in a sling.

"Almost," Billy said. "Can you bring Jessie to me?"

"She knows," Doug said. "I don't think she'll see you."

"She has to."

"You don't know her like I do, Billy. When she sets her mind to a thing, there's no changing it."

Billy turned his eyes to his foot and concentrated on the wound. The bullet had sliced its way between his second and third toes, causing a lot of pain and bleeding but no serious injury.

"I'll fetch some bandages," Doug said. "It's best you stay a day or two."

"If Jessie won't see me, I'll be off today," Billy said. "The foot won't heal for weeks. I know it, and so do you. It won't stop me from riding, though. Tell her, Doug. Please?"

"I'll try," Doug said. "But if it was me, I wouldn't count much on her coming down."

Doug brought a washbasin and several

bandages. Then he left Billy to bind the wound and continued upstairs to see his sister. Voices could be heard from upstairs, and Billy hoped that all would be forgiven. Doug returned alone, though.

"She told me to tell you everything has already been said." Doug tried to hide the sadness in his young eyes. "You aren't welcome here anymore."

Billy's lip quivered a moment.

"Wait at least a day or so, Billy," Doug said, grabbing Billy's arm. "I know you only did it for me."

"I did it for all of us," Billy said. "It was bound to turn out this way. Rest the arm, Doug. And take care of her."

"I will," Doug said, extending his right hand.

Billy shook Doug's hand, then allowed the boy to burrow his face into his chest.

"You were supposed to teach me to shoot," Doug complained.

"Well, I don't suppose we have time now," Billy said, smiling. "Do something for me, Doug. Post those letters."

Doug nodded, a sour look on his face. "Jessie said they were in case you died," he said.

"There are lots of ways to die, Doug," Billy said somberly. "Billy Starr did die in that street a few minutes ago."

"Maybe when I'm a little older, I can come out to the mountains. You can teach me to shoot, and we can build a cabin. How'd that be?"

"Sure," Billy said, brushing a tear from Doug's eye.

"It won't be the same here when you're gone," Doug said, finally stepping away.

"Not so many windows to replace, huh?" Billy said, forcing a smile onto his weary face.

Billy paid a couple of farm boys to load his chest onto Comanche's back, then supervised the lashing himself. Billy finally climbed aboard Bluebonnet and turned the horses west. As he passed the church, he glanced back at the mercantile. He couldn't help remembering other partings.

It was Ellen all over again, but this time he was filled with a feeling of hopelessness, a despair that swallowed his spirit. He could see Doug's young face in the doorway, could see a single hand waving farewell. But there was not so much as a crack in the upstairs windows, not a hint that an offer to stay might, after all, be extended.

So he was alone again. He nudged his horse along toward the open country that led to Colorado.

"Wonder who I am now," he said to the wind.

It seemed to moan an answer. No one. Nothing.

A man doesn't need much in Colorado, he thought. Not like in Texas, where there are land titles and big houses. In the high country a couple of good horses and a gun that shoots straight and true is enough.

The whine of the wind seemed to answer him again. It brought back memories of the Powder River country. An earlier moment came back to him, too. There was the solitary figure of a boy standing beside an old Comanche chief and his son atop the spirit cliffs. Below them churned the great rolling waters of the Brazos.

I knew a man named Fletcher once, he thought. Jack Fletcher. It's as good a name as another.

And so it was that Jack Fletcher rode off toward the plains of western Colorado, leaving behind the wide-brimmed white hat and the reputation of a man he'd never chosen to be. And with the departing hooves of two proud horses, Billy Starr came to an end.

With the ending of one thing should come the beginning of another. But there was no beginning in the heart of the man who rode away that morning, only a sense of something lost, something that had slipped between fingers grasping desperately for it. It was that terrible word, that shadow of a thing a man knew to be belonging.

Without it a man was doomed to be no more than a tumbleweed cast to the whimsy of the prairie wind.

THE END

Other titles in the
Linford Western Library:

TOP HAND
Wade Everett

The Broken T was big. But no ranch is big enough to let a man hide from himself.

GUN WOLVES OF LOBO BASIN
Lee Floren

The Feud was a blood debt. When Smoke Talbot found the outlaws who gunned down his folks he aimed to nail their hide to the barn door.

SHOTGUN SHARKEY
Marshall Grover

The westbound coach carrying the indomitable Larry and Stretch headed for a shooting showdown.

FARGO: MASSACRE RIVER
John Benteen

The ambushers up ahead had now blocked the road. Fargo's convoy was a jumble, a perfect target for the insurgents' weapons!

SUNDANCE: DEATH IN THE LAVA
John Benteen

The Modoc's captured the wagon train and its cargo of gold. But now the halfbreed they called Sundance was going after it . . .

HARSH RECKONING
Phil Ketchum

Five years of keeping himself alive in a brutal prison had made Brand tough and careless about who he gunned down . . .

GUNSLINGER'S RANGE
Jackson Cole

Three escaped convicts are out for revenge. They won't rest until they put a bullet through the head of the dirty snake who locked them behind bars.

RUSTLER'S TRAIL
Lee Floren

Jim Carlin knew he would have to stand up and fight because he had staked his claim right in the middle of Big Ike Outland's best grass.

THE TRUTH ABOUT SNAKE RIDGE
Marshall Grover

The troubleshooters came to San Cristobal to help the needy. For Larry and Stretch the turmoil began with a brawl and then an ambush.

RIDE A LONE TRAIL
Gordon D. Shirreffs

The valley was about to explode into open range war. All it needed was the fuse and Ken Macklin was it.

HARD MAN WITH A GUN
Charles N. Heckelmann

After Bob Keegan lost the girl he loved and the ranch he had sweated blood to build, he had nothing left but his guts and his guns but he figured that was enough.

SUNDANCE: IRON MEN
Peter McCurtin

Sundance, assigned to save the railroad from a murder spree, soon came to realise that he'd have to fight fire with fire, bullets with bullets and death with death!